To Pam + Tom

— more of the same, but
concentrated.

— Spam

EX LIBRIS
TSM

ALSO BY W. M. SPACKMAN

Heyday

On the Decay of Humanism (Essays)

An Armful of Warm Girl

A Presence with Secrets

A DIFFERENCE
OF DESIGN

A DIFFERENCE OF DESIGN

W. M. SPACKMAN

ALFRED A. KNOPF   NEW YORK   1983

THIS IS A BORZOI BOOK

PUBLISHED BY ALFRED A. KNOPF, INC.

Copyright © 1983 by W. M. Spackman
All rights reserved under International and Pan-American
Copyright Conventions. Published in the United States by Alfred
A. Knopf, Inc., New York, and simultaneously in Canada by
Random House of Canada Limited, Toronto. Distributed
by Random House, Inc., New York.

Library of Congress Cataloging in Publication Data

Spackman, W. M. (William Mode)
A difference of design.

I. Title.
PS3569.P3D5   1983   813'.54   82-48873
ISBN 0-394-53130-2

Manufactured in the United States of America
First Edition

To

Laurice

. . . My Lord D. has given over variety,
and shuts himself up within my lady's arms.

—Sir George Etheredge,
in Ratisbon,
19th December, 1687

A DIFFERENCE
OF DESIGN

1

Was it I wonder when I turned round, there in the car, and found him gazing straight at me.

The sun in his blue eyes. This American five minutes before I had never even seen.

Blandly looking at me.

And had been looking. And in that way. At I suppose my shoulders. At the soft curls at the nape of my neck. At where I am kissed.

And, now, straight into my eyes. The sun hot on his fair hair, the car's top down in the lovely day.

With from either of us not a word. And as if, there between us, suddenly there *was* this not-a-word.

Tranced almost, the blaze of summer morning everywhere.

—Except of course I simply disavowed it, ah mon Dieu *oui!*— simple and faithless as bonjour, as who hasn't to be!—anyway the warm wind of our speed was flipping and fluttering the sober stripes of his tie, so simply I murmured, "Chad is blowing us to bits d'you mind" as if that had been all, and let my eyes half smile at him for a moment, then I turned round front again, away.

Not that that helped.

We were hardly out of Versailles. All the way down into Normandy he was going to be there still.

Though heavens what if he was!

All the same I should not have let it happen.

—Though as if it mattered! Because alors bon, I am sometimes careless. And it was the suddenness of it. And the surprise, the unexpectedness. But I do as I please with them don't I always? And no matter what? For I do. I looked at Chad, the sun in his charming eyes too, and I said to myself, amused, on est lamentable.

—Still, it was careless.

I had merely turned round to say I've no idea what to him.

Nothings; the civilities one does. Chad had of course said what this Mr. Sather of his mother's was like, but what was he *like?* So this day at the manoir was to see for myself. We would pick him up in Versailles on the way.

Then I turned round. And he was gazing straight into my eyes. In silence. And as if somehow straight into *me*. I felt—I don't know how I felt! It was so utterly upsetting from what I'd turned round for, that I couldn't think what it had been I was going to say. I felt as if no man, ever in my life, had looked at me like this. And for just that one wordless moment too long I felt myself gazing back at him. As silent as he. And he knew.

—Ah, but knew what.

For in the courtyard of his hotel, five minutes before, when Chad fetched him out and across to me in the car in the haze of summer morning, what had there been to make anyone think there could be, ever, anything to 'know.'

He was a man like any other. Tall élancé easy urbane. For an American, not un-elegant. Comme un autre. Disabused-looking. A little I thought wary-looking too? A *little* greying. Really I felt nothing much about him one way or the other. And now in five minutes am I so uneasy, I said to myself, shocked, that I can't think what I could merely turn round again and say to him?

I felt I was—I could not understand *how* I felt.

It was as if he— It was as if that terribly self-assured gaze had somehow— But was I some helpless savage, tranced by the spinning of a sorcerer's wheel?

—I felt as if suddenly my neck and my shoulders lay naked. I was appalled.

He could reach out I said to myself and touch me and I could do nothing *nothing*.

—I needed *time!*

So I looked at Chad and said, *"Hé!"* mindlessly, and at least he said, "Hé yourself," the way he does. So at random I said, "Mais il est bien, ton homme," and if the man understood French, tant pis.

—I should *never* have let it happen!

We were nearly out of Versailles. I thought should I get in back then? Chad could stop. But then why shouldn't I have straight off, at the hotel?—what had changed? And he would know.

—Except Dieu du Ciel, I thought almost wildly, am I to put helplessly *up* with this? and I turned round smiling, arm along the back of the bucket seat, the leather warm on my arm in the sun, and said *poor* man I was thoughtless, I should have got in back with him at the hotel, he looked *deserted*. Still it *was* hardly an hour's run, did he know Normandy? our part of Normandy? we had this lovely domaine in the Bourgthéroulde area, a forest, wild boar and other gros gibier in quantity still, did he hunt in the States?—thinking how can I *bear* myself and this torrent of inanities on and on, under that bland gaze. . . .

But then there we were at the autoroute, and Chad was gunning his precious Jensen up into the cent-quarantes, we *were* being blown to bits, and I could shrug and smile excuses helplessly and turn front again, and slide down deep into my seat out of the wind, as if into a shield.

—There are no shields. I shut my eyes and thought in a kind of horror what have I let happen to me.

For what has there always been *there*, between me and any man, that so frightens me is not there now?—that *is* there, between a man and a woman, to be oneself behind, and safe! and I thought of Grand'mère's cool voice reminding me of *la barrière des bienséances, ma chérie*—though 'proprieties'? when even thinking about what I was thinking about was 'abandoned'! And a 'barrier'? that after five minutes I can feel is no longer between? I was in total dismay—for was I to think I *wanted* to turn round as it shocked me I was in dread this unknown man was willing me to? *Wanted* to look at him and have him look at me? I could not remember that he had uttered a word. Oh or I given him a chance to! and I *heard* myself babbling! That, dissemble?—I only just stopped myself from whimpering aloud.

Suddenly Chad whooped his "Porsche suisse, taïaut!" and I opened my eyes. We shot past the thing; but the wind of our swerve snatched at my skirt—and voilà, my dress ballooned wildly up before I could hold it. Chad cried, "Hey *hey!*" in his happy voice, like a tally-ho that too, and flicked a laughing look at me, and of course we both thought—it was a phrase of ritual by now; every time, it had been, since that first time on the road to Dreux—we both heard in our private memories the *What de good word, pretty britches?* he'd called out in the delight of our new nearness then, that first time, and I had let my dress balloon as it pleased, to indulge him. And now he always said it when it happened, it was like Swann's cattléyas, only this time we of course just thought it.

Lunch, we'd been going to, that day, at Dreux; and I'd let it balloon for him, and he shot the Jensen off onto the shoulder in a crazy shrieking of brakes and scatterings of gravel and grabbed me, and kissed me and kissed me till I lost my breath being kissed and laughing at him, I thought isn't it enough mon Dieu that I've acquired of all possible savages an American, without the creature's being enthousiasmé into the bargain? Grand'mère would have disowned me!

I looked at him now through my lashes, remembering back before that; and I said to him in my mind, I was behind *you*, mon beau hobereau, the first time I found myself wondering about you. Baudouin and I had hardly known you a—ho, was it a month? yes, because it was after Easter, coming back from Venice we ran into Jock Bingham in Aix and he introduced you. Then back in Paris it was that day Baudouin drove us all out to Raizeux for lunch, and Jock and I sat in the back, and I was behind you. And I began to look at your shoulders. And the nape of your neck filled the collar of your shirt so round and white, the skin such satin my fingertips almost felt themselves touching you, ah felt what it would be like touching you, the fair hair beautifully trimmed and short, just I thought where the bend of my arm would come, wound round, smooth as the smooth hollow of my arm holding you, mind you *all* this time chattering to Jock about n'importe quoi, heavens the things I think of! But I thought them; and a dreamy part of my mind was seeing how it would be, how we would be, you were taller so with my arm there my lips would be where? against your creamy throat, the taste of you on my tongue, and I thought for the first time in so many words Am I d'you suppose going to find myself making love with this man before long? for heavens perhaps I am.

But then *this* I thought is how it happens? As light-mindedly as *this*? Tiens, and as pitilessly! Can the rules one has lived one's life by become, in the flicker of an eyelid, the mask of one's disguise instead? as without a pang one forswears what it was! I looked at

Baudouin's handsome head, and without a pang I saw the salon of your flat in the Avenue Bosquet, hazy with the gold of early summer that afternoon he and I first came to tea. Jock was away. Was away, I remembered you said, often; and there in my husband's car, driving to Raizeux, I looked at the handsome column of my husband's neck, not one whit less charming mon bel américain than yours, and with a little shock I found I had begun to plan.

—Months, it had been, since then. A year nearly; and now that was how I felt this silent man was thinking about *me*. I could not understand how I knew. And if I turned round where could I look but into his eyes, and he would know I knew, I could not keep him from knowing. I felt how terribly near he was—*no* barrier, *nothing* between—he had only to stretch out his hand. I knew of course that he would not: they do not, ah *no!* Ah, but if he should?—for this man was I felt closer to me than any man had ever been or I'd thought could be, it was as if in a dream I found myself in a terrifying world which had rules I had not been told and had been forbidden to ask, and I said to myself if he touches me what *can* I do?

Nothing. No matter what, nothing.

—But to sit *still*, being touched? . . .

Yes, but to turn round, admitting it had happened?—there *was* no way to deal with it! And he had not spoken a word. He had not had to. And I said to myself, in horror, this whole day lies before me, in which there will be nothing I can do. . . .

We shot past the exit for Mantes. I shut my eyes.

—I could not go on like this.

Except I thought but am I totally out of my senses? for why should I have to 'do' anything! They enter our tastes, yes; they can enter into our feelings till not a word need they say of what they are thinking, to make us in our folly believe we know, and that it is what we want it to be. But *I*, have I not always more a disposition to appraise, say, than be tender? And is a quarter-hour of folly to have changed me?

D'accord, I was careless. Hoh, but is that a change?—how many another time too haven't I been careless! And why in any case should that be an entrée dans mes goûts, much less dans mes sentiments? I remain Me.

And voilà, all at once I *was* myself. I opened my eyes and looked at Chad, thinking how aimable to be adored, even simplemindedly; and I said to him—as good as flippantly, I felt suddenly so gay—I said, "Tiens, maybe I like you for reasons I can add up!" laughing, and if he had no idea what I was talking about, poor sweet does he even when I know myself.

But when we leave the autoroute for Louviers, I said in my mind, I will turn round. Without a tremor.

Because this American, after all!

It was only because Chad hadn't said *this* was what he was like.

—Though of course we hadn't discussed him very much. Or very long. Or even why he was here. Just at the very end of that lovely afternoon two days ago, Chad's rooms all soft early-summer nightfall already and I was thinking I must go, I was going to Maman's for dinner, she'd said *don't* dress ma chérie, you're coming up from the country just come straight here; but from the country I'd have allowed leeway, so I said to Chad, "You're making me late," and sat up. The room was filling with dusk, the tall windows were no more than frames for the fading day beyond, and in the depths of the pier glass I could just make out the gleam of my reflected body, silver against the shadowy room behind, I was leaning on a hand over him, looking down, 'musing' he used to call it, 'ton petit air d'en rêves' (he *is* so sweet, all he will ever need is someone to adore him) " . . . making me late," I said, "and we haven't even

discussed what to do with this Sather of yours, what *is* he like?"
Because the man had it seems arrived days ago. We weren't in Paris.
But now we were, we couldn't *not* meet him. Or put it off.

Of course Chad said what was anybody like? fingers lazily trac-
ing my thigh. Sather was a Wall Street type, how not? A well-turned-
out perhaps-fifty. Been he thought widowed; urbane diner-out type
anyway. Entirely presentable. Une personne de condition.

I said, "... Coureur? Comme toi?"

A chaser at *fifty?*—though of course anybody he supposed why
shouldn't he?

I said, "But so *family* an errand," watching his face. "You don't
think perhaps he's her lover?"

He snorted *god* no! in amusement—*his* mother with a lover? I
was out of my lovely head. Sather *advised* his mother, was all, in-
vesting. In and out of the market as well as solid long-term stuff. So
he was coming to what the profession called 'look into' him.

I said, "*You* an investment?—hoh!"

Ah, well, his mother was in the habit of 'retaining the services' of
anybody and everybody. Meaning she ordered them formidably
about. Why doesn't Chadwick come home when I tell him to? Mr.
Sather, go find out! Is he gambling? Is he Entangled? "Sather's here,
madame l'adorable comtesse, to rescue me from *your* lovely clutches,"
he finished, snickering, and tried to pull me down by him again.

I thought how silly. I tucked my toes under me and knelt up
and away from him, stretching, watching my image in the pier glass
arch her slim back and reach her pretty arms high in the dusk too,
fluttering her hands at the tips like flowers. We yawned. "Sous mes
griffes, how *really* silly," I said. "Are we to— Should we *do* something for the poor misinstructed man, to amuse? ..."

(Even, I said to myself, pour lui plaire. And control. For why else was I trained to please?—as only, really, I suppose, my light-minded ancestresses and I have ever been trained to please.)

So we'd decided, have the man to luncheon. At the domaine. Feed him, and see.

For I thought ah mes belles aïeules how straightforward being alive must once have been, au grand siècle. Woman or man, the scenario was dans les règles and foreseen. And the rules were like the stage directions for a masque at court. 'Quand l'amour se déclare, une femme vertueuse'—the very style as good as falls into formal verse. When love speaks, a virtuous wife 'lui impose silence.'

Imagine.

And silence imposed not because the declaration has upset her, but because she has made it a principle for herself that it is upsetting. And so (logically) she resists because resist she must....

Ah but the trouble can be, by resisting one can drift without knowing it into the taste for adventure that resisting adventure brings. What charm in the virtuous sentiments she's resisting with! What a high-minded romance they create to play a part in, to adore being the heroine of! And meantime the lover, asking forgiveness for having upset her, upsets her all over again with the passion of his excuses—and how natural the rules make it seem!

And one found oneself excusing his passion—for how deeply sincere it must be to overcome him like this! And how star-crossed and unhappy he sounds—and can it be only rhetoric, that no beauty on earth but one's own has caused it? We fall into a kind of wonder at how noble his sufferings are! And how like our own! And it is our virtue that has caused them!—until suddenly, hoh! we no longer have any, and all that's left us is the virtue of lamenting its loss, oh *really* what a marivaudage!

The green-and-white *Sortie Louviers 1000 M* shot past, and

Chad began slowing for the turn-off. I looked at him and almost laughed. For enfin what a consolation in one's ancestresses' day too the sheer good manners of one's undying remorse les règles made possible. Even one's frailty, mon Dieu what a word, all the same they said it!—even one's 'foiblesse' was excused by the virtue of one's sad self-reproaches. In fact, I said to myself as Chad skidded us off into the exit ramp, every advantage of virtue a woman has went to the profit of her misbehavior.

And thank Heaven still does. I sat up and turned round, and let my eyes smile at this dangerous new American of mine, and I said to him, as bland as he, "See what a bad place for you France can be Mr. Sather?—Chad's learned to drive like a frenetic Frenchman."

But what I thought am I doing. It is not safe. Especially it is not safe unless one *knows* whether one is throwing down a gantlet or what Grand'mère used to call 'letting fall a lavender'd glove.'

Not that what *does* one ever do with a man but one or the other! And what help is it knowing which?

And I don't know which anyhow....

—Yes, but until I do?

Should I try simply boring him? If only because mightn't it make him seem safely boring too?

I could prattle us into a polite stupor with, say, a set-piece history of the domaine. Ah but Mr. Sather (I could say) how I do adore the place, the great beech forests, the wooded rides opening on and on and on, it used to be one of the royal maisons de chasse. One of my light-minded ancestresses adored it too (I'd say)—at any rate she was it seems unusually kind to one of the Louis, was it Douze? *totally* kind and I suppose as often as necessary, goodness the things one did, anyway she got it out of his Orléans clutches. And into ours, what heaven. Commodity for commodity. Isn't 'in kind' how you say it? And, well, she *was!* Though she'd have said 'en nature' wouldn't she, how amusing. Or d'you think there's all that difference Mr. Sather. . . . Heavens how common I could make it. But I could set my teeth and do it couldn't I? 'Oh I must show you a portrait of her in the petit salon, Mr. Sather. A *lovely* commodity, one hardly blames the king.'

Aïe.

—Though of course instead of this we were gazing into each other's eyes with every just-met politeness, and disposing of the pre-liminaries.

A banality was a banality but had he found Paris amusing?

Amusing himself, he said he was sorry he had to say, hadn't been what he'd come for. It was only a brief mission anyway. To oblige a client.

But not, surely, evenings too?

Oh, well, evenings, he said smiling, evenings no. Evenings he'd taken advantage of a very agreeable guide-and-escort service he'd had the good luck to be put in touch with. Astonishing what you found existed, in large cities; but it seemed there were several of these agencies in Paris, with a staff of well-brought-up young French or American women who'd show you round. *Entirely* formalized and proper, need he say, but they looked after you. Where to eat, what there was to see, what to do, what not to—a sort of spiritual chaperoning generally. So, anyhow, this young woman he'd been as-signed, a Mrs. Godfrey, had been very kind indeed for his evenings. Gone to the opera once with him. Gone dancing with him too, a couple of times. Couldn't have been kinder.

These people in fact looked after you very well in general. The Paris hotel for instance he'd stopped at first—she'd said how did he expect to put up with these faceless international glass slums? the

Empress Eugénie had of course lived there, but that had been a *long* time ago, and, well, was what they'd done to it since to his taste? so she'd immediately moved him to this Versailles place.

And quite right—huge comfortable Edwardian bedrooms, and those enormous tubs in the baths: no comparison! Honorable kitchen too: did a splendid Sunday-lunch buffet among other things. Which he'd noticed a lot of the (by the look of them) local gentry seemed to turn up for.

I said but American young women went I'd been told into liberated rages, didn't they, if men treated them as commodities? So sad, too, somehow—when all we need do is look at you as if you were quite wonderful, murmuring *goodness!* at intervals.

—Banalités de luxe. But did he know enough my mind said to know what they were for. Years, it takes men, even to begin to try to see what we are like. Or as much as begin—so stupid. Still, this man had had time. Chad said he was fifty. Ah, and the kind of man he was anyway! I did not see how he could not be what I felt like this he was.

Or how any woman could not feel he was! And I thought and each of us in her time thinking, la mort dans l'âme, how many others must have felt as we, and against the hovering sweetness of his memories of them the very blandness of his gaze told us we were helpless—even, among so many so like us, were ourselves hardly a difference, so stricken, his power over us itself our dismay. For how strange if that were why I could still feel how frightening that endless stopping of time had been when I turned round. Or was it the panic of *being* frightened? for how strange.

Simply perhaps it is like that epigram of was it Madame de La Fayette's? that if a man has been loved often enough it is hard to imagine his not knowing it when he is loved the next time too.

For this man must.

—Except that it is a longer word than love.

Which Heaven spare me.

For ah it is like one's girlhood midnights again, writing à la chandelle a letter that even then one knows one can never send. *I am awake. Because of You. I know I should not tell you it is because of you. And oh I should not write it. But I am not sleeping. I am feeling. And I want—There is a part of me I want*—a letter perhaps it will be deepest dawn before one shreds it into a thousand tiny squares. But ah, one writes it; and *does* this man I thought know enough to accept it that banalities 'impose silence' as they should? Or does he know they do, but knows also what he is, and will not obey.

And need not, because I know he need not.

—Suddenly I could not stand it.

And I said to myself I *will* not! Let Chad take over the amenities! We're nearly at Elbeuf aren't we?—and in ten kilometers the lodge gates? Un petit quart d'heure? Let Chad take over the entertainment of this monsieur de rencontre!

Have I to go on trapped à deux like this as if there were no one else on earth?

The very look of it a symbol! ...

C'en était *assez!*—and in the middle of a phrase I simply turned round front again. In the middle of I didn't care what! *Away!*

I felt—I did not know *how* I felt!

—Or even, now, how I seemed to feel about Chad either, and I looked at him in dismay. At his profile, at the delicious corner of his mouth, the sun on his hair, the sun on his throat. His long fingers on the wheel. As if I had expected to find him somehow changed.

For did he look the same? but then of course I saw he did, and I thought oh how absurd anyway, how could I see him as different when how could he be, heavens—he is an era in the private history of *Moi, Fabienne,* is all, even if only an early one, que sais-je. Though if that was all, how at this era I should know it I did not see. But the definition amused me, and I said to him, "Tu as un air plus mérovingien que je ne t'en ai jamais vu!" and he could take it as he liked. But by this time we had got through the market-day noon traffic of Elbeuf and out onto the Pont Audemer road beyond, and I was myself again anyhow.

Then in no time we were there, as so many thousands of times I had been before, the huge old marronniers in flower still all the long avenue in to the lodge gates from the voie, the sun-flecked shade of the allée a tessellation of fallen petals, pink and cream, then the arched grilles of the gateway and Emile's Maryse waddling out of the lodge to kiss my hand and leer at ce beau Monsieur Newman again and swing the tall gates open, then the green shadows of the beeches through the parc, and then suddenly out into the white glare of the courtyard at last, the blaze of noon hot on the cobbles and the sun-drenched ancient stone of the manoir glittering up and up like a bastion for my refuge, and I was out of the car and up the perron and *in*, set free, ah how sweet a house, I was so light-minded and gay again that I thought ah zut why *not* show him her portrait, cette aïeule who so gentiment earned all this for me, and if he thinks I look like her, alors bon, I do....

And ah, moving about now I could look at him, no longer trapped à deux. I could *see* what it was that had happened. Or at least I said to myself I can look at him and look away from him and look back at him again as I please, and either way it will mean nothing at all, *nothing.*

So, then, presently, it was so green and lovely on the garden front I had Emile lay the table for luncheon out at the pavilion, in the little columned Roman atrium some grand-père or other had had built before it, the sun filtering down over us through the new leaves into wavering mosaics and patterns of light on the paving; and as we sat down the brilliance of early afternoon lay on the lawns, and down and away to the pièce d'eau and the water stair and the carp pools at the woods' edge beyond, spilling the glint of the stream into the dark vanishing aisles of the beeches at last, where the forest closes in around again.

And at least mon trouble . . . wasn't it lessening?

For what was there to think I must 'decide,' here between them in this heavenly day? mon beau hobereau d'amant and my—this— Oh *really* how could a man like this one have undertaken any such opéra bouffe of a mission with a straight face! What possible description, even, was he expected to present the situation to me with —'sous vos adorables griffes, madame'?

But then instantly I thought, and it was like a small cold hand closing about my heart, But *is* he perhaps as blandly cynical as that, as *heartless?* Like a gleaming mirror the glass of the table-top threw its patterns of leaf-shadow like veils of silver light up into his face, into his eyes, he was talking to Chad smiling, winkings of sun in the green gold of his wine reflected up too, and I looked at him and thought is it happening to me all over again, that dismay? For what am I to do, seeing him again—as how am I not to, if I am why he has come. Chad it is of course he was to talk to. But if he should try to see me too? Even if merely to repay this déjeuner. For if then I am alone with him, eyes in his again across a restaurant table? Or there beside him on a banquette, a few mere centimeters away? . . .

He was telling Chad of a visit he'd made to the Normandy battle-fields. Filial piety, he said amiably: his father had been wounded there, at a village called Saint-Sauveur-le-Vicomte. Name of the place had so amused his sergeant, theologically, that the fellow hadn't kept his eye on a German patrol. He'd visited Omaha Beach too, a wild day of scudding cloud and onshore gale, the Channel a chaos of toppling combers; spume and spindrift flying. He had left his car by the voie and slogged across, and come out through the dunes into the loneliness of the empty sands. Mile after mile, and no one. And nothing, only the endless thunder of the Atlantic tumbling and bursting on those beaches of desolation, and the bones of German blockhouses like great beasts stranded there, gaping, the beach-grass growing in their doorways. He had been absolutely alone, the salt spray stinging his face and eyes. He had *felt* absolutely alone. What had it been like there, that morning a lifetime ago. Gone differently, he supposed, from *his* war. Which had been he said Korea.

—Does he mean I thought la Corée?—with a shock, for what American war was this? Are there wars one doesn't hear of—or was this just before I was born. For how old must he have been? Though yes, if he was twenty in that war and fifty as Chad said now. Though *twenty?*—for ah what had he been like, young. *Then* would I have— Could a boy of twenty, even he, have so totally— But what if I had, and then he had been killed there. . . .

But the *death* of this man? If it were now? I looked at him through my lashes, and then at Chad, the sun-spattered shadows of summer veiling his blue eyes too; and it was not the difference of age between them but oh I thought how could anything be so not the same.

And I am not claimed.

—Though have I been ever. Or wanted to be.

And from always. Think how I used to sit, those endless dripping afternoons here at the manoir the summer I was twelve, sit at the portes-fenêtres onto the terrasse from the salon, dreaming out in a perfect little fillette fume at the rain coming down in long weightless lines across the mist of the deserted lawns. Or it would clear, and I would trail sulking through the wet green carpets of fern beyond the carp pools in the dusk, and watch the rimless violet of evening darken and fade away over the crown of the forest, *wild* that it was still not time for me to try my eyes on a man and see what would happen.

And so faithful to myself then too, ah mon Dieu what a little savage I was!—so myself already that I even knew I'd never have a passion for whatever lover I'd have fancied without having one too for a rival I'd have picked for him—if for no reason but to find out how it was, two of them! And what it would turn out they were like, to have, differently. And what I should find out about their lovely differences, like that. And oh miracle after miracle after miracle of possible chances!

Yes, and in what sense they would be my *property....*

But Dieu merci never I theirs!

And of course what *amusements,* for instance whether whoever it turned out to be would be like that husband I'd read about in was it de Gramont? who 'wasn't jealous but he always managed to be inconvenient,' and how did it happen if both husband and lover happened to be both.

—Only then, hoh, it turned out to be mon beau Baudouin, who is neither.

And from the first, was neither. Like me. Like all of us. I remember how he and I, at the bal de fiançailles—it *was* a heavenly night, deep country summer everywhere, the manoir like a great jewelbox of light, the whole front and the forecourt lit from high overhead in the dark air by the enormous porte-flambeaux they'd used for balls in Maman's day, and from the salon wing the marquee was like a great glowing ballroom built out into the night, its tenting lined with a deep green toile, that somber First Empire green, swagged and garlanded along the cornices with white, and the white of the fluted pilasters at the piers made whiter still by the soft pallor of the candles in the pier sconces, and down from along the high peaks of the tent the sweep of three great chandeliers, the facetted glitter of their lustres shattering light into thousands of disintegrating particles as it fled endlessly away.

And out on the gardens side of the salon wing the terrasse too was lit by a line of porte-flambeaux, their great guttering torches breathing a kind of luminous dusk down over everything; and we had the buffet there, in the warm night, the music drifting out into it from the marquee, muffled and sweet with distance, and coming through the grand salon between too.

And I remember how Baudouin and I stood with our parents at the salon doorway and thought cars would *never* stop arriving and arriving or we be free from receiving, it must have been two hours nearly we stood like good children there, for his families and mine, cousins and connections and friends, for generations some of them from back forever, those family worlds that had known us from childhood (the same, many of them) and from our pays around us and from Paris and the Midi, from London too, some of them; and my friends and Baudouin's, and a few of Baudouin's from back in his Charterhouse days—oh a company so long known, so kindly, so like us, yes and so timeless that somehow the evening itself might have been a kind of endless pause outside the accident of time, those hours like an island out of all our assembled pasts, an island so enchanted that we should never need to visit it again, and jusqu'à pas d'heure I danced and danced.

Oh, and the first cool pallors of summer dawn were there before it came to an end, the parc slowly filling with silver light, the last coils of mist seeping and sifting back like retreating ghosts into the dusk of the woods behind. The porte-flambeaux in the forecourt were guttering out one by one, high in the greying air, as the last happy babbles of adieux were being chanted, and then the echoes of the last departing cars died one after another in the distance away, and we were alone with the wakening rooks in the enormous stillness.

Over the terrasse the torches had burnt out too, when at last Baudouin and I kissed our parents goodnight, and went out for a last glass of champagne there. The tiles were glistening with dew, the first white-gold shafts of sunrise were just striking through the crowns of the great beeches behind the pavilion and up across the lawns into our eyes. It must have been almost four. I thought how many hour-after-hour men d'you suppose I've danced with, and Baudouin began humming that waltz from *Faust* and there I was in his arms again, drowsily turning and turning in the dew, alone the two of us turning in the wide world, goodness I was half asleep, my head on his shoulder, his voice in my ear sounding sleepy-happy too, and I thought what a darling, on a bien fait, and he bent his head and kissed under my ear, and down into the hollow of my shoulder and I heard myself murmuring, "Tu vas me séduire?" So of course he snickered, "Serviable!" that joke from our childhood, and I'd have snickered too except I was yawning; but I thought ah but the instant my head touched his pillow I'd be asleep, and I said, "Mais au lit, tu sais . . . ," yawning again, and he began to laugh at me, and then I was laughing too, it was hopeless, it was too sweet to be anything but hopeless, and finally we just took the last champagne in, to the kitchen, and I suppose what we had was breakfast.

—Oui, on a bien fait. And I know as much about him by now as I expect I ever shall. Or as much as one decently should. Or, really, want to—am I for instance to fuss guessing whether he has someone as I have Chad, un amour rangé of his? Or bother whether now and then he even has what Jock Bingham says they called 'bespoke sex' at the university? *what* a thing to waste curiosity on.

Not that I don't I suppose wonder whether Baudouin is ever

curious about me—in the sort of loving-onlooker way I am about him sometimes, making love. Because *I* am always alive to *any* change in rituals, in the way we do, there hardly ever are, but where there are my mind is *instantly* busy sorting and explaining them if I can and trying to fit them in. But why shouldn't I expect him to be as good at dissembling his elsewheres as I am mine? One is simply a little careful. Out of respect for each other. And for les bienséances too.

And out of affection, voyons!—un mariage qu'il a su rendre heureux.

—But then I did not want to think about what perhaps I should have to think about next, and there in the brilliance of early afternoon was Chad instead anyway. And his difference from Baudouin a difference I knew. Though how strange, when I thought back over it—had this changed what I saw the three of us as, à la légère, when it began? Because at the very first there I thought the difference was simply the, the, well simply the lovely breathlessness of it. The light-headedness, the freedom, the *delight* somehow—a rendezvous was the way dances were in one's teens, fête pure. And, well, perhaps they were, simplicities and all. Only then, except that Chad was Chad but Baudouin was Baudouin and my husband, was there the difference? Except of course that this time I'd carried myself over the threshold. And except that Baudouin naturally would always be there and I shall always expect him to be—c'était normal, we were brought up that way. Because whether or not one accepts it, one expects to behave as if one did. So if elsewheres are light-hearted, or even if only light-minded or just de gaieté de coeur, they are light-winged and fleeting too; and one returns. Never having, really, been away.

But now? With the difference of *this* man? ...

—And I sit here between them I thought in the long murmur of this day (and ah in what ways between them!) as if there were not this curtain about to go up, on a stage set for some lost comedy perhaps of Marivaux's, the set a garden front like this, of a manoir centuries out of time, the pale stone of its walls warm with the seeping gold of summer, the first soft shadows of afternoon already at their slow obliterating climb; and here at a luncheon table center-stage the three of us, each in his stylized part. But then how stylized a trio I suppose Marivaux might have seen us as, la ravissante comédienne Heaven pity her most of all—and not marivaudée but oh, beset! For à quel saint se vouer? And am I to know which way to turn either, better than she?

—And my sweet Baudouin, *now?*

What has happened to me what has happened to me.

—Ah mon Dieu mon Dieu I could not bear it! The sunlight was stifling me with gold, je me sentais *mal*—they must go, *oh* they must go!

And why care how? I stood up. And if Chad looked at me astonished, let him! They could think what they pleased! I would say goodby at the terrasse. Up the drowsing summer of the lawn I could feel Chad's concern, and I didn't care, dear God I had no strength to, *any moment* I said to myself I may feel that awful trembling start again. And what if, at goodby, my eyes say a helpless *Do you know what you have done to me?* to this man, and every moment I did not see how I could stand it until I could face what it was, alone.

—Except then, well, at the end he merely said something gallant and smiling about 'enchantment,' and I smiled back into his eyes as if there were nothing but bienséances in the world, and said, "Or do you just mean that women are habit-forming."

Silence imposed.

It was dawn when I woke. The cool early light was drifting in through the hangings of the bed, and I lay and watched it slowly fill the dusk of the canopy above me with white shadows. The lovely stillness of country-summer morning was everywhere. I must hardly have slept an hour.

—Though then how could I have slept at all.

For did I ah even believe in what, finally, I had decided? when it was a longer word than love?...

Qu'importe, it was decided. Or at least the démarche decided on. Even, of a kind, a schedule. I looked at my watch; it was not even *five?* Hours still, hours, before I could reasonably try to phone. And begin.

Except even then.

—Well, but at least, soon, Emile's boy would have been for my baguette for breakfast. Alors bon, I would dress for town before.

And then not *wait*. I could phone on the way. The poste in Elbeuf is right on the voie. Or at Louviers, just off. Or I could leave the autoroute. At Mantes, even.

And I could phone the Embassy before I left here, to have Jock asked to expect me.

—Was it going to be hot? I went to the window. The first white blaze of sunrise was just beginning to glint and dazzle through the tops of the beeches, but the whole wide sweep of the lawns up to the terrasse below me was silver still with mist. A heron stood motionless at the far edge of the pièce d'eau. I watched the pure crystal light grow and unfurl and deepen in hue, and suddenly, on the sundial, the first glowing shaft of sunrise burst through the treetops and struck the tip of the gnomon with golden fire, and then, ah how lovely, along the whole dawn-shadow rim of the parc, bar after glittering bar the saffron light fell slanting through and up the lawns, and slowly the floating radiance of morning was over everything.

I lay in the bath thinking what to wear. It was going to be hot. The sleeveless white shantung? Or was it in the flat in Passy. Over the bathroom's Venetian window a mourning dove roucoulait on the parapet. How the doves had amused Chad. "But they're *French*-speaking!" he said. In the States they coo it seems differently. He was so funny about their 'language problem'—if one tried to cross-breed them would la jolie petite even understand qu'on lui faisait des avances? Would the squabs be bilingual?—would they feel cultur-ally disoriented and not fatten properly?... How long ago that was. Early on, between us. His first visit here. Poor sweet. 'Once upon a time.' Comme dans les contes de fées...

—Yes, but also 'il était une fois' you too, ma belle, I said to myself: once upon a time (remember?) earlier on between us still, you too in idle amusement were wondering, for mightn't it perhaps put one out, making love in English?—the whole au lit vocabulary of your Frenchness translated? *redefined* even, in barbarisms? Aïe, and suppose in American it was différent still again!

Heavens, the things one thinks of. And then, hoh, how it turned out instead.

—I had breakfast on the terrasse, the lovely morning already hot and still, the sunflooded stones of the manoir behind me tower-ing up against the blue glaze of the sky. A hawk was wheeling, high over, his pinions scattering sapphires of light. Or was it a falcon. The heron was gone.

—But how was I to wait. I was too upset. I took my coffee into the study, and rang the Embassy.

Could I leave a message for Mr. John Bingham. It was urgent; would the standardiste have the great kindness to *make sure* it was handed to Mr. Bingham himself the moment he came in? Could he be told, please, that the Comtesse de Borde-Cessac wanted, d'urgence, to be able to get in touch with him. She would phone again. Between nine and nine-thirty and would he please wait for her call. It must have been a new standardiste: I had to spell my name.

It was not eight yet when I ran down to the car in the forecourt. The house was still pointing its stately shadows; the cobbles were wet still with dew. Elbeuf and Louviers would be much too soon to phone from: Jock wouldn't nearly be in. I decided to make time and phone from the poste in Mantes—nine-fifteen, nine-thirty. And in my mind as I drove off into the sun-spattered ancient aisles of the beeches I saw him in his immaculate office, the soft Parisian morning floating in through his windows over the Rue Boissy-d'Anglas; and perhaps he would be in his shirt sleeves at his desk, he might when I called be dictating dispatches or memoranda to that creamy secretary of his I'm not sure doesn't sleep with him now and then, well he is tempting, why shouldn't she, and at the standard they would put me through to him and he would pick up his phone.

And there would be his nice voice, perhaps concerned: "Fabienne? Angel what's wrong!" and I would say, " 'Wrong'?" and he would say, "But here's your switchboard message saying it's d'urgence," the girl's dark eyes watching him. But I would just say, "Oh, that," but so he could take me to lunch, heavens. I was coming up to town. And then we'd discuss where.

Or he'd say, "But 'urgent' lunch?—*serious* eating, this is for?" and I'd laugh and say, "Well, and Embassy rumors"—because are 'calculated indiscretions' his special Embassy job or aren't they. And he would give that engaging snort of his and say something like "*That*'s not the d'urgence I take women to lunch for!" and the girl would laugh.

—But all the same, d'urgence it was.

Because ah poor Chad. Because I am not heartless, I am *not*. Except how was I even to put it, I thought, mon Dieu how did one *do* it! I drove on and out and onto the voie, and off toward Elbeuf through the lovely fresh green paysage of morning, and for a little all my mind seemed to see was the Avenue Bosquet, those rooms for so many light-minded months at least some sort of a part of me, even the salon hazy with the amber of afternoon that first innocent time Baudouin and I went there to tea, but then room after room to the very last one, which who could have guessed was the very last, or a symbol, that bedroom in the summer dusk only three days before; and I said to myself but am I then really not ever going to step across that secret threshold again?—or, I suppose, tell why.

Or *is* this, merely, the way it happens. And has to.

La terre écarte de sa face
Ses longs cheveux indifférents—

who reads Pellerin now but who cares? and I remembered how Chad once said to me *Grâce à toi l'univers s'explique*—so sweet and simple of him. Ah well he is simple. And I may as well admit I've known a long time.

But does one feel one's 'plus jamais' no more than this?—or had I simply no other emotion to spare for Chad, no passions de reste, in this nightmare of dismay?

I who had been so politely astonished, so often, at what other women do!...

And what had been the *use* in saying *I must not decide, I must not look at this man*, when oh Heaven help me just saying it was deciding!

Ah mais regarde-moi—regarde comme je fais.

—But I *need* never see him again.

He will leave. He will go back to where he has a milieu. To his Wall Street; to his Maine coast in the summers. For what meaning has France ever had for him. He came now only as a courtesy to a client. Why should he come back, ever? There is nothing for him to come back for. Even if he knew what has happened to me, there is nothing. For I would not see him. All the more not, if he knew. If I don't dare risk seeing him again now, why would I then. I would not. Let me not, now. Oh let me not need to. Let me not think he is ever likely to return. ∘

Let it not be catastrophe. . . .

—Ah, but wasn't the proper prayer, I said to myself, 'Let it not have begun'? And had I decided not to see him again or hadn't I? With nothing more then to remember of him, had I to dread the days to come—five hours remembered of a summer's day the only meaning of a lifetime? *I* forlorn?—that at least I shall have stopped short of! to have had nothing was at least that much un bien.

And if I find his flowers I thought in the Passy flat when I come in this afternoon, and presently he rings up, as he may, to ask to see me, I have only to say no. And that my husband is coming on a fortnight's leave from his regiment, I didn't know his plans but I rather thought we were going off to—well, wherever came to my mind at the time. And it was partly true. For of course Baudouin *was* coming on leave. And I *didn't* know whether it was to be Portugal.

And he was going to be my excuse for Chad too.

—Jock was waiting for my call. *God* yes he'd feed me lunch, what a question! Where'd I thought of going? because look, sweet, would I mind Barbizon? That Bas Bréau place, say. He had to go on to Fontainebleau at four, was why. Line of duty—had to see a man about a spy, very stealthy stuff. Sure I wouldn't mind Barbizon? I was a pleasure! The Bas Bréau then? Quarter to one?

I came out of the poste into the morning street again thinking an hour and a quarter to Barbizon leaves two hours still to fill somehow. Off toward the Seine, a few streets away, the twin towers of the cathedral glittered above the red-tiled roofs of the town: I could go light a candle. And watch it burn slowly down.

Or I could drive into Paris and have Jacques do my hair. He would work me in.

Or I could go to Passy. But what if Chad phoned while I was in the flat. Every morning he does. And I am not, well, not *prepared* yet. And there would be the flowers from— Ah but what if I had to face finding he *hadn't* sent them.

So finally I just drove in and went to Fauchon and took a *long* time buying all sorts of friandises. To be sent to the flat, for Baudouin's arriving.

And I went to Hédiard too and bought things.

And on my way across Paris to the Porte d'Orléans I stopped to light a candle at St.-Germain-des-Prés and left by the Porte d'Italie instead.

I was *not* heartless! I was not a Mme. Récamier and Chad would not be a Benjamin Constant lamenting her in his tear-sodden journal day after day after *day* till Napoleon came back from Elba and distracted him.

And Constant knowing exactly what she was doing!—'she doesn't want the nuisance of feeling sorry her charms make me suffer so, so to spare herself she thinks they don't.' *Pour s'en délivrer elle n'y croit pas.* What a sentence.

But then what a woman. And how did she put up with the man, even for his political usefulness. Heartless or not.

I could not have been like that even if it had been that sort of affair. Or of ending.

—I was ten minutes early in Barbizon, but sweet Jock was there.

Jock Bingham has always charmed me. Of course he was Baudouin's friend first, from lycée days. And it was Jock's father's sending him to Charterhouse that made Baudouin want to go there too. But now he's—this last year in particular—he's more mine. Even, perhaps, just mine. He was standing waiting for me in the court of the Bas Bréau, elegant as usual, in a white linen gilet croisé this time of all things, with jet buttons, and he came across to the car with that kindly air of his of being put-upon-but-I-was-worth-it, his repertory of worldly divertissements mine to command, and he'd begun amusing me almost before he'd ordered apéritifs.

For would I believe what his high-minded dedication to his country's diplomatic competence had just involved him in? There he'd been—(What did I see I longed for in the menu? He hardly thought that duck aux ananas!) There he had been, after my phone call, blamelessly letting this British legal chap from next door start the daily wasting of his time—and with some memorandum of livery of seizin who on earth cared *who*'d endossed on a deed of enfeoffment, except was it authentic ("What am I, the College of Heralds?") and *only* this godsend prospect of lunch across a table from *me* was getting him through the first horrors of Embassy morning (Look, how would I feel about sharing this filet en feuilleté pour deux with him? And what to start with, then? Argenteuil asparagus? Or was I seriously hungry—when *had* I had breakfast? before I'd called him?) when his phone rang, and it was this Yale professor who was a visiting world-authority on American literature, at the Sorbonne, and so help him the poor learned idiot was gobbling with fright!

And there was this kind of wild happy singing going on in the background, and once it had come sort of swooping in on the phone and then off and melodiously away—no wonder the poor sod was practically hysterical, 'd unnerve anybody—anyhow in God's shattering name would somebody COME AT ONCE!! Because this student of his, student also of his it seemed back at Yale but she'd followed him abroad, well actually she'd more or less come abroad *with* him—anyhow half an hour ago she'd suddenly gone completely out of her head, and he didn't know how you— What were the proper French —Because good *god* it had never crossed his mind! Student infatuations of course yes; perfectly routine campus behavior; old story; girls *did*. But then this one had— Well yes recently he'd begun to notice she, she'd taken to sort of humming. In he meant bed. You know?—*not paying attention*. And then, this morning (and right in the middle of!) she'd—well she'd burst into song!...

Ah, well, Jock said, he supposed nobody was very sensible sexually. Think of some of Stendhal's behavior. Think of Tolstoi's. For that matter think of some of God's. But he'd loyally trundled round (for what else? she had our passport hadn't she, baying mad or not?) he'd trundled round to this incompetent rake's apartment and sure enough there the child was, swooping about, waving the chap's pajama trousers if you please like a heraldic banneret, in the full lustre of her lunacy. Fey, he'd decided, though, perhaps, rather than strait-jacket barmy. But what a commentary on the mating habits of the race of man. Was one to call it dejecting, or just hilarious? He'd said to the dithering Yalie, What next what next, didn't he ever check with the college psychiatrist before he got into bed with them? and all the ungrateful lecher'd done was snarl, "None of your philandering damn' business!" and rush off to lecture on (he said) Poetic Strategies in Elizabeth Bishop.

So he'd rung the Assistance Publique. And packed an overnight sort of bag for the child. And fended off a couple of giggling attempts to garrotte him with the pajama trousers. And rung the Embassy to give the boys time to handle the damn' thing. And in short he'd preserved the consular amenities until the Assistance Publique had turned up and lugged her away. Singing of summer in full-throated ease.

What next what next indeed.

So that had been *his* morning. Such as it was. Thank God for *me.* I was a lovely giddy creature to feed lunch to and now what did I want him to tell me about this chap Sather.

—For an instant I thought I was going into shock. *How* could he have known? Or guessed! And when I had been so certain I would be safe that I already thought I was. . . . It was so dreadful that for a moment I didn't see that he wasn't looking at me, he was running his eyes down the wine list, ah *I was safe* and I said the first inanity that came babbling into my head, "Don't I have any surprises for you at all?"—and I even managed to laugh.

And he merely glanced up amused and said what surprises? because look, it was only yesterday I'd met the guy, and fed him Chad said a very decent Pays de Caux lunch hadn't I? but then, this morning, the Embassy switchboard time-stamp recorded that I'd rung *him* up for God's sake at 7:19. But why on earth, at that hour, call him at the Embassy and not the Avenue Bosquet? So what *had* I wanted to discuss out of Chad's hearing? Simple! Hardly needed to wonder.

So of course I said heavens what was there to wonder about, I'd merely wanted a third opinion. Je lui avais trouvé du charme, à ce Sather. But why would a man as civilized and as sympathique as this take on such a—in 1983!—such a really preposterous mission, heavens! Or was he did he think as cynical as it made him perhaps seem?

But Jock said oh come, what did I want the man to do. You couldn't very well explain even to an Iowa client that she was an anachronism could you?—simple question of manners. Maybe in Iowa she wasn't an anachronism anyhow.

Sather'd he said turned up looking for Chad the morning after he'd arrived in Paris. It was a Sunday; he'd been lazing around in the apartment, and Sather'd stayed a good hour and filled him in. He'd it appeared been looking after the Newman family's investment portfolio for a good many years. Even made them money before this latest consignment of nonentities brought their cracker-barrel economics into Washington. Investments, and then inevitably you found yourself being asked to look into other areas now and then as well. Especially now it was just Mrs. Newman. Would he for instance find her a religious broadcaster to buy for tax purposes (but *not* one of those smarmy or whinnying ones). How *much* money, please, should she expect to have to put up with Chadwick's wasting at Princeton. One became resigned. And actually, Sather had said he felt, there was a sound financial side to it anyhow: high time this young man started thinking about coming home and taking over a few of the dynastic chores. How much longer was he going to put it off? Good god, what was he now—twenty-seven? twenty-eight? . . .

—It was as good an opening as any. It could have been exprès. So I decided; and I said, "But sweet why do you suppose I rang you. For a long time I've been thinking shouldn't he go."

Oh, of course I oughtn't perhaps to have said it quite like that, it did sound blunt, saying it—and he *was* absolutely taken aback. Hoh, I thought, so I do hold surprises for you! All the same, was there any real use in 'explaining'? So meaningless, when what would it be but the classical situation, tiresomenesses and all. With nothing new either side could possibly have thought up that hasn't been thought of and said from the beginning of time, pointlessly pointlessly. . . . He would say but the poor guy adores you! And I would say I know I do know, and he *is* so simple and sweet, and Jock would keep repeating his baffled irrelevant but *adores* you! and I would try to go on sounding meek and to blame and dans mon tort in general, I've no idea *how* many times I might have heard myself murmuring I do feel badly, I do (because I *did!*), perfectly senseless all of it.

So I simply told him. Tout passe, voilà. In a new love perhaps everyone is innocent; then each couple creates its sequences for itself. "I'm turning classic comédienne for you," I said—but thinking of Chad, remembering how it began, that long-ago afternoon, how breathless he was, half afraid of me, he couldn't believe I was saying yes, even when he kissed me he could hardly believe it; he was shaking so, that first time, I thought was it going to be a fiasco? maybe I should soothe him somehow?—except I was so wild myself I could hardly wait till he touched me, for how would it be? and how afterwards too would it be, adultery, all these years from my girlhood wondering, and now I was to know....

But now here, I said to Jock, tout passe; and wasn't this Mr. Sather here with the answer? Anyway *an* answer? "So I rang you first," I said.

So he took a long breath, and said, "Well, God bless God bless," looking resigned. "I'm to give Sather a hand? On souffre courageusement son bonheur!' You are an absolutely adorable woman and I never blame anybody for anything. But thanks to your adorableness I have been for a year now in a totally impossible position. Now at least the situation is to be demoted: I shall be a mere retrospectively uncomfortable. And being tired of Chad I can see. Mais autant que *ça?* ..."

—That at least thank Heaven I thought is what I want the reason to seem to be. But ah did it make it any less sad to put it in French? and I said, "Oh Jock but in French how does it sound."

"Ah, well, dammit, 'quod vides perisse,' then," he said, "over's over, what's the advantage of having classical tags on the tip of my tongue if I'm going to be astonished at anything as immemorial as woman?—what you've collectively sworn to us the winds and the waters carry away. Ventis rapiuntur et undis. And always have been. Look, angel, I call this a gloomy conversation, let's for once have an overpriced Clos de Bèze and be done with it."

So I could laugh at him. "But men recover," I said. "All you need is someone to indulge you if you're simple-minded. Or over-indulge you if you're not," and he said lightly, "Oh, epigrams," and signaled the sommelier.

But I went on to what came next. Had this Mr. Sather said how long he was staying?—did he I meant expect to take Chad back with him. Because how was he managing, with no French. And only this escort service he'd said he'd engaged; this young woman.

Why, Jock said, these agencies, he knew of two or three of them, they did a very competent job, why not. They were a sort of very superior couriers; they took people about. There was supposed to be nothing they didn't know. Including how to keep their clients from committing the next shattering American bévue. Very businesslike. And charming. Very expensive of course too, but the stockholders foot your bills.

I said but couldn't the situation become, well, ambiguë? Mr. Sather's young woman had for instance he'd said changed his hotel for him. And she had gone dancing with him. Several it sounded times.

He said what was her name? he knew several of them. They turned up at the Embassy with clients. Who was this?

I said a Mrs. Godfrey I thought.

Maria Godfrey? but he knew her quite well!—'d met her at parties as well as around the Embassy. *Very* pretty girl. Even deli-cious. Sather *was* in good hands!

I said stupidly he'd said she was very correct.

And of course he laughed at me—what'd I expect? some sort of what his stately grandm'ma used to refer to as 'a lightskirts'? Look, these were—they *had* to be!—jeunes femmes sérieuses. Divorced, most of them, to prove it!

I said well yes I'd wondered. About I meant this Mrs. Godfrey's husband, if she went dancing with clients every other night. And then, well, I'd wondered what kind of expatriate life a young—of course it *was* I supposed a way for an American girl to make a living in Paris, but didn't this Mrs. Godfrey—

But simply it's good god he said a country you like existing in! Drawbacks of course—our intellectuels with their sub-Heideggery fads and sweeping nonsensical aphorisms. Where but France would you hear a Jean Rostand announce 'L'homme est un miracle sans intérêt'?—all right then what *does* interest the fellow! We sometimes struck him as being out of our over-Cartesian minds. Or again: would *any* other nation put up with the suffocating ronds-de-cuir bureaucracy we French did? Still, that was qua citizens. Qua *French*, everybody but the bourgeoisie let everybody else do anything their anarchic fancies suggested to them. So American girls could be themselves here (or for that matter be anybody else they pleased too) without having to strike liberated attitudes about it. And an American writer, say, could sit over a bock half the day at a café table, writing up his personal improvements on the Book of Revelation, and nobody would think it worth a glance. Or a waiter hover. Whereas at home the poor devil would have to earn his unappetizing living teaching freshman-english.

—How quietly, I said to myself, I sit listening to him. I might be that marquise of Musset's—je commençais à avoir trente ans. But how can he tell me what I can't let him see I want to know. And when I haven't 'decided' anyway.

I thought of Fontenelle: 'Wherever there are men there are follies—and the same follies.' Except Fontenelle didn't dignify us by saying *folies*, he said *sottises*.

And poor sniveling Constant bore him out: 'Les femmes m'ont fait faire tant de sottises.' Tiens, how thoughtless of us to trouble men's peace of mind so! . . .

—Ah, but it helped, that lunch! Jock amused me. And cheered me. If only with other people's sottises. At a nightclub he'd heard one of those fluting English voices at the next table—"one of those lovely delinquent ladyships, and she was complaining to a sleek solid guardsman sort she called Arthur about some chap she called poor Charles. 'I said to him, "Oh darling *could* you find it in your heart to just *go away*, I mean *not* fussing about it my very sweet? because I'm afraid you're beginning to give me what may turn out to be the horrors." He was rather put out. Such vanity—what things you *are*, Arthur!' "

And he told me about a folly an old uncle of his in Fiesole had had built, in his grove—a "heptastyle tempietto, its seven sides expressing Uncle Robert's contempt for astrology and his personal independence of the points of the compass." And for all he knew some anti-Palladian notion of where to make love. It had turned out to be rather uncomfortable: his uncle'd finally had to have central heating put in. "But much superior anyway to one a Main Line cousin had had built," he said. "*That* had a stock-ticker installed."

And there was a young American studying piano at the Conservatoire who was making a *very* good living composing demotic ballads for a dive in the Rue Vavin—

> I don't want no mo sweetie-pies
> Ef all they is is you

and so forth. And something called Bach Rock for variety.

And, oh well, Jock is good for me. And désabusé. And for dessert we had fraises des bois.

And when he put me in my car he said what time is Baudouin getting in, and I said for dinner I hoped, and he said how long'd he have this time, and when I said two weeks he looked at me and said blandly but I *was* going to be busy? And I said I expected so, yes. And he said but only perhaps part of the time in Paris? And I said yes we might go to Baudouin's father's, on the Corniche. Or to Portugal perhaps. We'd talked about both. On verrait.

So he hadn't to ask whether the Avenue Bosquet would be seeing us. Which was the message.

And so he smiled at me, and patted my hand on the wheel, and leaned in and kissed my cheek, and I drove away.

That much taken care of.

But we shall all (I said to myself as I drove back along the autoroute)—we shall all need time.

Day-after-day time, too, to grow used to this—to what has happened. Dear Heaven to its *having* happened! Time simply for me to revive from that in!

And for Baudouin perhaps without knowing it to grow used to how I may be until I do. For how *do* I make love with him now. . . .

I drove back to Paris fast. Baudouin might have wangled an earlier plane. I wanted to rest anyway. There was . . . the night ahead.

And it was just as well I did drive fast: at the flat there it was, waiting, a great floating armful of flowers, and an engraved card saying MR. LEWIS LAMBERT SATHER.

Without another word.

2

Ms. Godfrey tilted herself up over him on an angel arm, and said in a happy voice, "Let me contemplate you"—for they had seen no real point in getting up, it being Sunday.

So, for hours, from the blaze of morning beyond the slatted shutters, bright motes of sun had chinked and filtered in, myriads, her tall room swam with the glints of their floating patterns, and, now, they were sifting with the brilliance of, outside, practically noon.

But since why should this young woman now some five days his have expected an answer, he only took the wrist of her free hand in his fingers, and lazily kissed it, instead. At which, as having no other amusement at the moment anyhow, they both then smiled.

Till at last she murmured, "No but I keep wondering what you were like, when you were only I mean my age," as in dream. "Are you likely to have been rather a pet?" she added, and bending kissed his chin.

Oh, Sather said, been he supposed like pretty much anybody. Undifferentiated marauding pre-stuffy East Coast near-thirty male then; how not. Something of a bastard now and then too of course, like anybody in his right mind. Why bring his that-stage up?—'d give *any* decent man the horrors, remembering, good god!

" 'Remembering'?" she said, and watched his face. "Like what?"

He appeared to think. Ah well, he said, after a moment, unkindnesses, mostly. Inadvertences. What had he known, young! Why didn't she come down again where she was convenient.

But this she paid it seemed no attention to. Or for that matter moved; but, poised atilt there, over, bent her enchanted head as if musing upon him, cherishing, this long fathomless gaze down.

So they lay there, half tranced, faintly smiling still.

Till at last, from those depths of dream, she murmured, ". . . must get *up*," not stirring.

He made a lazy expostulating sound: 'up'? for what for.

"You make love instead of lunch *too?*" she protested, laughing. "Goodness!" and, bending, kissed his eyes.

So, naturally, like a man of sense, he pulled her down beside him again. Where she lay, giggling.

"Floreant Gadara by god anyhow," he said (thanks to a decent Quaker education), and stroked her sleek shoulder.

Or was what she'd been trying to say, he added presently, that he was keeping her from mass.

Suddenly there was silence.

She reproving him? he asked, sounding amused.

She seemed, minutely, to detach herself from him; but she said nothing still.

So he rolled up onto his elbow and looked at her. This some technicality'd escaped him? he asked blandly.

"But Lewis you must know," she gently rebuked him. "One doesn't take communion when one's doing, well, what I'm doing, sweetie *anybody* knows that!"

This was for god's sake *sin?*

She have to confess it even if it was?

". . . But Lewis the priest would think it was if he knew," she said meekly. "And it would be a *discourtesy* not to think of his feelings, can't you see?"

The fellow's hypothetical finer feelings, hypothetically well yes, he saw. But how was a poor heretic to follow the niceties of this sort of thing? Because he said look, they were a wonderfully confusing collectivity and what was one to do? He remembered one otherwise tractable girl who wouldn't even consider making love Sunday mornings, because that, she said, was when you went to mass. This, mind you, wasn't because the lovely thing *went* to mass Sunday morning. No no, simply she wouldn't come make love during the time she'd have been at mass if she'd gone! She conceive of such bedlamite piety?—the one perfect time, too, when her damn' husband wouldn't have suffered uneasiness! Two perfect hours (counting to and from) just thrown away—the sheer *inhumanity* of the waste! So now how'd she expect him to— And don't flounce! he cried, and held her—look dammit he wasn't talking about the girl, he was talking about theology pure and simple, this was lofty speculation, built-in superstition or not, he told her, practically as if he expected her to agree.

So she lolled back against him again, and gazed at him, close beside, lovingly. "Do I have to hear about your horrible other girls?" she murmured, and putting out a fingertip traced the line of his mouth. "And anyhow," she said gently, "it isn't superstition. Le bon Dieu has been very kind indeed to you, my love, and so have I."

But so Old Testament hit-or-miss! he said. He put it into the head of an Iowa Baptistess that her son's virtue must be saved from a life of lobsters and fancy women, then persuaded of all people *him* to undertake the cockeyed mission—but to what end? *Her!* Nothing, he agreed, could have been lovelier—Aphrodite herself couldn't have been more thoughtful! But so roundabout, so *inefficient* somehow! God was good, of course, but He often didn't seem to be all that good at it. *Was* she going to tell her confessor about this? . . .

"Are you stupid?" she cried. ". . . and anyway it's my religion and *my* decision, and if I decide to passer huit jours avec un monsieur it isn't really the church's business at all! You don't know anything about theology anyway. Did that girl confess about you?"

No idea, he said.

"Didn't you ever ask her?"

Why should he have!

"But you asked me!" she accused him.

. . . Different girl entirely.

"How, 'different'?"

How'd *he* know how? he complained amiably. Simply not this lovely dazzle, call it. Never set off rockets in him this way, if she liked.

"*Not* just my Sunday-morning difference?"

He said good god no! as blamelessly as if this were so.

So she kissed the corner of his mouth. "Are you perhaps sort of lying a little?" she asked tenderly.

But didn't she take that for granted? he teased her, and ran the tips of his fingers up through the slipping shadowy tent of her hair. If she expected anything as far-fetched as truth from him, how would she decide which parts of it she wanted to believe?

"You haven't even learned what I want to hear?" she asked, nuzzling him. "Or do you just think I'm so light-headed about you you don't have to bother?"

'Bother'! he echoed—'*bother*'?

"Oh well and anyhow," she said, "if I decide to lavish myself on you that's *my* decision, Lewis my pet, you have nothing to do with it.

Except, I hope, go out of your mind over the total sensuality of it," she ended, little tongue lightly savoring him.

So they lay there in great comfort, and they might simply have been mindless.

But presently she said, "I do think you're silly, sort of, though, to call her again."

A try, he said. Like any other. Because no telling.

"But sweetie, this lunch," she said. "D'you really have to? You've met Mr. Newman's poppet, and she turned out *not* to be a poppet, she's a perfectly ladylike countess. And rich. And you sent her your thank-you flowers. But then when you rang her up and asked her to have lunch with you she said, politely, no. And isn't that that?"

Put that way, he conceded, yes he supposed very likely.

"Then my silly love what can you expect from ringing up and asking her again."

Ah, well, he supposed he had some vague feeling he ought to apologize somehow. Good god, now he'd met her, he not only didn't disapprove, he was all for Chad! And for all *he* knew, she might want to marry him; divorce what's-his-name and marry him.

"But ces gens-là don't *divorce*, heavens!" she said. "Any more than they emigrate or abjure! They think it impious and vulgar."

He meant apologize for the, the affront of his damn' mission. Not of course in so many words—words would only make things worse. But just sort of—

"You mean *charm* her?" Ms. Godfrey demanded, coming up on an elbow to look at him. "Oh dear have I a rival?"

He said oh nonsense—when she'd said no to lunch with him? God no, he didn't think she'd even particularly liked him. Could have disliked, even. No no, all he'd wanted was to, well, close the whole implausible incident with the routine civilities of regret, what else was he to do? Merely, say, leaving a card struck him as pretty damn' bleak. Or did the French leave cards.

But she was gazing down at him as in total disbelief. "Oh *really*, Lewis my darling," she cried, "how can you have the, the effrontery to be so bogus modest!"

But what was he to think.

"As if privately you thought *any* woman would 'not like' you!"

He made some vague grumbling sound.

So for a moment she appeared to contemplate him. As being possibly beyond interpretation.

Then she began to laugh. "Because know what would serve you right?" she asked sweetly. "Because I'm supposed to *advise* you aren't I? and help you carry out your ridiculous mission efficiently and everything? Well why don't I advise you the *efficient* way to put a stop to Mr. Newman's truancy would be simply for you to supplant him in the lady's arms! And don't look shocked, my heartless pet!" she cooed at him. "*You* object to another seduction-campaign more or less?—hoh! And in such a worthy family cause, too, goodness!"

So, shocked (or perhaps in fact not), the man seemed not to know how to take this, though who would.

And finally merely remarked (mildly) that any man was, naturally, only on loan so to speak anywhere; but, well, she surprised him.

"Ah *do* I!"

Or did she mean she'd eventually want him back.

" 'Back'!—if you'd done a thing like *that*!"

All he'd meant was—

"Make love with another woman and come back *expecting* I'd simply—"

But dammit he'd—

"Oh well never *mind!*" she said in a voice of tears. "Except you are sort of heartless anyway aren't you? and now you as good as threaten me with— And don't say 'It's just a lunch'!" she commanded, and took herself out of his arms altogether. In fact sat up. "You don't know anything *about* women! It was at lunch *I* started falling in love with you, don't you know that? Or anyway at dinner, so there!"

—And now he hadn't even let her eat breakfast, he said, amused, what behavior! and rolling up after her took her in his arms again. Where at least she had the complaisance to giggle.

And in due course say, "All right *go* be unfaithful then!—now are you happy? And why aren't you starving too," she complained, and kissed him. "So let me go. Where did you throw my— Let me go!" she reproached him, kissing him again.

And so forth and so on.

Except that, presently, at the bedroom door, for an instant she turned and looked round at him, smiling. "So I shall want you back," she said in a happy voice again, and vanished toward her kitchen.

These two, then, were at least past any stage at which lovers, abed in gratitude and wonder, recite to each other, in alternating song, the Arcadian miracle of their ever having met; and it had been a good ten days. Counting anyhow from the first.

When out of the brilliant noon of the Rue de Castiglione she had come into the cool glass depths of his hotel so light and quick she was at the concierge's desk asking for him, spun round in fact and halfway across to where the fellow pointed he was sitting, before it seemed he took it in it was he, Sather, she must be heading for— hardly given him time to scramble himself to his feet before there she was, smiling as if delighted into his eyes, slender gloved hand out to him.

And a beauty.

Though this it could have been thought he had clearly not counted on, for he looked, in a courtly fifty-ish way, for a moment as good as wary.

But she was lightly chiming a well-brought-up "Mr. Sather? oh how d'you do I'm Maria Godfrey, but you've been down waiting for me how *kind*," in a voice of music—for how pleasant to be *meeting* at last, lunch instead of just telexes! so now where did he want her to suggest they might go? Or had he perhaps somewhere he'd heard of in mind? as one did!

For in case *not* (she had run on, wide eyes softly taking him in) she'd thought why not Drouant, they were very good again, also it was only this ten minutes' walk away, did he know the quarter? in the Place Gaillon—they could simply stroll there if he liked (they'd be early anyway) through the noon streets in the lovely day, would he care to? for she had reserved a table, in case.

Unless of course he felt too fagged to?—after she meant his plane.

Though he didn't in the least *look* fagged, she told him, for an instant all eyes at him, in fact he'd go beautifully with Drouant, what a pleasure to have so presentable a client (sliding a hand through his arm as they took off), did he know Paris?

So through the glowing maelstroms of Parisian noon they had sorted out the polite preliminaries.

No he'd somehow never got to Europe. Even in college summers. His father had had a big yawl; they'd cruised off the New England coast, summers. Up into the Maritime Provinces; that sort of thing. Then, his service had been Korea, not Europe.

No she lived in Versailles, not Paris. *Far* more square meters of apartment for so many fewer thousands of francs. And then one could commute in to *either* station, St. Lazare or the Invalides, so handy.

And so forth, along the Rue Danielle-Casanova. (No, not *that* Casanova, that was Giovanni Giacopo. Jean-Jacques. Like Rousseau. Terrible male chauvinists both of them, so *silly*.) Shops yes, did he want to buy presents for friends, before he left? she'd shop with him, she loved it. But *this* wasn't the quarter to, they'd *shop*. And across the Avenue de l'Opéra and there they were, and she was translating the menu to him (in detail) over a glass of champagne.

For was he hungry? For how hungry? Though in any case he should have a Drouant sole; everyone should. She, though, was going to have what they called a 'mignonnette de Pauillac,' it had a heavenly tarragon sauce; he would see. But the carte des vins didn't need translating, would he order. And, please, another sip of champagne.

And so, as the sommelier bowed over her, competently around to business.

For he knew what their agency *did*, that part of their set speech she could skip; but also she was supposed to tell him about herself, they'd found it was only sensible. Just people were curious, and why not.

"So then I've been I explain married," she told him. "Only that turned out to have been stupid, too soon after college like everybody, so I am divorced. And then *I* add," she said sweetly, "I add 'But I don't have a lover. *Nor* am I looking for one.' There, that's the other part of my set speech—not that you really in the least look as if you needed having it said to you, Mr. Sather, I mean do you?"

He had murmured, looking amused, why, he hoped none of his fellow clients ever'd needed it said to them either.

"Ah, well, sometimes, no," she'd said. "No, it can even seem safe sometimes to add 'I love being charmed.' If one of you, that is, looks charming. Still, every now and then it can be a *little* like handling one's father's classmates at reunions. You know? in their various happy stages of dignified rut?"

But good god, he'd said, and he might have been as courteously shocked as he made it sound, good god what were he and her agency's clients like then!—they lunge, and that sort of thing? to have called for *this* kind of cards-on-the-table warning-off to him!

"Oh but heavens," she cried, "I didn't mean to *alarm*! What sad primnesses have I put in your mind, Mr. Sather?" she begged him, laughing. "Oh *dear*!"

Not that he'd blame some poor greying devil, he'd said gallantly, for being—what should he call it? 'over-enchanted'? Certainly he himself hadn't had the pleasure of taking anyone this lovely to lunch, he hoped he might say, for blest if he could remember how long.

This however she had passed over with a bland *poor man how deprived-sounding*—except 'enchantment' wasn't, was it, what he'd come all this way from New York for, even if his letter hadn't (for whatever reasons) quite seemed to her agency to say what the object of his trip in fact was. They were after all a guide-and-escort service; what was it she was to guide-and-escort him into? Or was it out of.

So, before the sole even, he had got down to it.

Well, no, he'd said amiably, perhaps he hadn't been all that specific, no. But the fact was, to put this particular scenario in black and white on the letterhead of a serious-minded investment counsel— Well perhaps the way to put it was just that he was indulging a rich client. A Mrs. Newman. Very rich in fact—widow of Newman Industries. They made couplings; huge plants in Burlington and Ottumwa. Which she had stepped in and run after Newman's death with a rod of iron. *Extremely* strong-minded woman. And used to giving orders. And she had this truant of a son.

Who had she said spent *quite enough* time dawdling about
Europe since college. He was to *come home!* And take a responsible
part in the dynasty! But what was she to do?—the miserable boy
didn't answer letters. *Or* cables! And his phone wasn't it turned out
listed! So would Mr. Sather have the kindness to go find out what
was going on? and put a stop to it! And *bring—him—home!!*

Ms. Godfrey murmured, "Goodness," politely.

Well, yes, mothers, Sather'd conceded: a certain cultural lag.
Still, he remembered young Newman as very good-looking, last time
he'd seen him. Could have done with a bit more Eastern polish,
perhaps. But some engaging young woman can always decide to try
buffing you up for reasons of her own. So, conceivably, Mrs. Newman had a point—for all he knew, in Iowa that stern-minded
archaism 'an unfortunate entanglement' might still be current
English. Chad was creeping up on thirty anyway—old enough *not*
to have to know better.

"But what has this wayward Mr. Newman been doing then?"
Ms. Godfrey asked. "Or do we know."

Sather said what difference what. Been at one point he understood studying architecture. Or some such intellectual pastime. At
he thought Urbino. But latterly just, well, it seemed here in Paris. No
idea doing what.

"No but I mean," Ms. Godfrey had said, "isn't this all rather—
You don't seem to me to be at all the sort of— Oh dear I guess I
mean isn't this all Mr. Sather rather *personal* I'd have thought? to
call in an agency like ours over!"

Been Mrs. Newman's idea. Though why not—he had no French
to get about with. None since college. And there were all the un-
familiar foreign logistics in general.

"But why hasn't she simply I mean come herself?" Ms. Godfrey
asked, as why not.

But what if an 'entanglement' (Sather said) was what Mrs. Newman was upset she might have the outrage of finding if she came?—and of having to confront! And dear god suppose the delicious entanglement didn't speak English! Look, he'd said, forbearingly, even when *he* was an undergraduate some of these musty tropes were still around. You could even be *expelled* from a college in those days! There was even such a word as misbehavior!

So she smiled at him over the rim of her glass, sipping.

And said, "But still, how do you, well, *feel*, Mr. Sather, about it."

How'd she mean. Because as one male about another, if Chad was a marauder or whatever that generation called it, well he supposed who wasn't. Not the point anyhow. And no concern of his if it were. But as the family's money-man, family firms he had to say made him uneasy. In principle; but in particular when they were this sort of autarchy. Because lose the autarch and you never knew about the financial viabilities. There could even be for instance no market in the stock! He'd seen such situations, and they were very unsettling indeed. So it was *very* much in young Newman's own long-term interest to get back and into the thing himself. Should have done long ago. And avoided *this* nonsense!

Ms. Godfrey murmured, "... couplings," as if lost in dream.

But then here the waiter began serving them. So this they watched.

Though then she said, "Yes but I meant *is* this all there is to it, Mr. Sather? Here you are, going after a wayward son practically as if you were part of the family. I'm not prying, goodness, but we've found we can be more efficient for our clients if we do know the ins and outs. Office politics, you know. And other kinds of emotions. Well, we are expensive, and here *are* we really needed—so I mean could Mrs. Newman be just giving you a fond and luxurious vacation as much as getting you a disinterested courier. So for example does she perhaps want to marry you or something?"

He snorted *god* no!—not even something, looking amused.

"No but is there some reason she mightn't want to? I mean, you can't be all that modest, can you?"

'Presentable,' huh? he said.

"Well aren't you?" she said sweetly.

Ah, well, he said, Mrs. Newman was a, was an unusually able woman, should they leave it at that? If she'd ever been farmington'd into an Eastern deb type, it hadn't taken. In a word this mission was just a mission and no complications, except the damn' awkwardness of it, and he hoped she and her agency would accept it for what it was.

"Alors bon," she said. "Simply then Mr. Newman is a promising young man a wicked woman has got hold of, and you have accepted the mission of separating him from the wicked woman. Oh dear, it sounds practically like a novel we had to wade through in American Lit, Henry James or somebody. Are you quite sure she's bad for him?"

He'd no idea. Might even be good for him. Could have been adding refinement that had been a good deal wanting. There *was* very likely something to be got from lobsters and fancy women, if you had time on your hands.

"So then how do you propose to handle it then?" she said.

Could hardly make plans could he? until he'd seen what was in fact happening. Too many unknown factors—Chad's attitude; what his young woman was like; whether she might be a young man instead; the current state of the attachment. Which for instance might turn out to be on the wane already. So he'd thought he'd reconnoiter perhaps first—at least get a working notion. But *not*, if she didn't mind, this afternoon—always had to catch up on his sleep after these barbarous planes. But he might drop past in good time in the morning. Perhaps she'd have the kindness to pick him up at his hotel afterwards, for lunch? Then they could start to work out what it was he'd found he had to deal with.

So then that, roughly, was how they had left it that first day.

⌒

But when next day she picked him up and drove him out through the immense wild vortex of noontime traffic to Versailles ("This is a hotel Mr. Sather I do think you'd be far more comfortable in. I want you to see."), first thing he had to report was a damn' nuisance but there turned out to be a hitch—Chad wasn't in Paris!

Nor immediately expected back, according to a young chap it appeared shared his apartment with him.

He'd asked the hotel concierge was it far, walking he meant, for he'd thought why not; and as she'd know, it of course turned out to be an easy twenty, twenty-five minutes, through the fresh Paris morning. And easy to find—the fellow had whipped out a folding map and spread it, to show: diagonally across those gardens, then this Place, to the Rue St. Dominique, and along it five hundred meters is the Avenue Bosquet intersection, had Monsieur a particular address in mind? because it was simple, street numbers everywhere began always from the Seine.

Ms. Godfrey murmured except when the Seine wasn't there to begin from.

Yes, well, however it was. 41-bis had turned out to be seven or eight stories of massive poured-concrete Modern; seemed to be standard for the neighborhood. Wrought-iron grille of a portal, flush with the pavement; and behind, this broad low-vaulted passage, practically a tunnel, led far in, over cobbles; it could have been a carriage-entry. Through the gloom he'd seen, as if distant, the haze of summer morning in a great cube of a central court, and a fountain, a grotesque stone lizard dribbling water into a flat basin. One of the grilled gates stood ajar. He stepped through, saw what he supposed must be the concierge's lodge to one side, and rang the bell. There was an aroma of something wonderfully appetizing simmering. From the court he heard, faintly, a piano doing Baroque cadenzas: somebody was playing with a window open. He waited.

And was about to ring again when this stringy little woman in a grey smock came scurrying out of the court and down the passage toward him. Jingling a great ring of keys. Gabbling God knew what. Ms. Godfrey murmured, "Oh *poor* Frenchless ambassador," she should never have left him!

Anyhow he'd finally made out, he said, that it must be the sixth floor at the rear of the court he wanted— Nieumann oui oui oui oui mais oui *là!* or some such, and he had crossed to the entry. High up over somewhere the piano was spilling this glittering allegro down through the sunny air; Haydn, it sounded like, or Mozart; notes like handfuls of facetted jewels; showering down the elevator shaft too as the glass cage rose with him smoothly up and up nearer through the spirals of the surrounding stair, and when he came level with the sixth floor, it turned out that was where it was coming from. And when of the two doors that faced across the landing he rang the one whose card read BINGHAM/NEWMAN, sure enough the piano broke off in the middle of a bar.

So what to expect he'd no idea. He waited.

But at once the door'd been briskly opened, and there was this tall suave young man with a cup of café au lait in one hand and half a croissant in the other. He had nothing but one of those loose towel-robes on. And was chewing something. He gazed amiably at Sather, mumbled "Mouth full; sorry," politely, and went on chewing.

Sather told Ms. Godfrey it had rather taken him aback. So he'd filled the interval: afraid was he disturbing him? forgive him, his name was Sather and he was looking for a Mr. Newman. He was a long-time friend of his family's, and he happened to be in Par—

But "Mr. Sather good god *yes!*" the fellow'd interrupted (having meantime it seemed swallowed), "you're this kindly ambassador we've been threatened with—or is it seen as a Mission? God bless me how d'you do I'm John Bingham. And you meet me at my cleanest. As you can as good as see. Come in, sir, come *in,* Chad I'm sorry's out of town for the moment. But at least this morning," he'd run courteously on, and led him in, to a long sunflooded room where a girl (in nothing but a loose towel-robe either) sat at the keyboard of a grand piano, staring at them—"*this* morning we can offer the local amenities of woman and song. In one delectable package. Miss Barretts is studying at the Conservatoire. And happens to be at *her* cleanest too. As, again, you can see. Or partly see. Or do I mean see in part. Barretts, this is a Mr. Sather, of New York, de passage for our improvement."

The child looked at him with great golden eyes, and said, "Hullo," through a yawn.

"Will you listen to that?" cried Bingham, as if in delight. "Who says women don't reward effort! A mere month ago, when she came floating into the Embassy like Spring in a Botticelli, all she'd have said was Hi. In fact it was the first complete sentence she ever addressed to me. But now by god give me till Bastille Day and we'll have her saying How-d'you-do as if she'd been born to it!"

"He doesn't approve of being from California, is all," Miss Barretts said, to Sather. "He says it disinterests him. Venery, what heaven."

She pushed the piano bench back and came gracefully to her feet, the folds of the robe still more or less around her.

"All *sorts* of things can disinterest him," she went on, to Sather.

"You've got to be lucky he let you in at all. You know what he did the other day? the other day a couple of perfectly *sweet* young missionaries came to the door and said, 'We're Mormons,' and you know what he said? he said, 'Why bring your spiritual misgivings to me?' and shut the door in their faces! Well nice met y'by," and trundled off.

At the door, she turned and looked back at Bingham. "Your *friends!*" she giggled. And vanished.

"*That*'s how things are," Bingham said amiably. "And as for the foreseeable future if it's not Freud at our case-histories it'll be Bowdler. The content, sir, is the all—take some heavenly creature to see the Sainte-Chapelle and she'll want you to explain the plots in the stained glass to her! God moves in His customary preoccupied way, tossing off universal truths at random intervals. Or quoting St. Paul—far and away His favorite author. In a thunder of Sinaitic platitudes. But here, sir, dammit, what am I thinking of!—what can I do for you?"

And in short, Sather finished it, with a mild snort, the visit had been preposterous from the word go.

But Ms. Godfrey murmured, "Oh *dear!*" as if stricken.

So naturally Sather looked blank.

But what was she to *do*, she *knew* Jock Bingham! she as good as lamented. She saw him all the *time!*—clients wanted things done for them at the Embassy, and that was Jock. And she saw him at parties! She'd even danced with him, and here Sather was giving her this—this—did she mean unbuttoned or unbosoming? view into the poor man's private life, how *perfectly* awful!

So about all he could say was well God bless.

Well she should think so!

Though how was he or anyone, he protested mildly, to have expected the damn' world to be so small.

But *this* sort of coincidence!

But he said but not really, considering her job and Bingham's?
—and Chad an American? Simple matter of course. As had sharing
the apartment been, for that matter, according to Bingham. One day
a couple of years ago he'd happened to drop past the consulate
downstairs on his way out to lunch, and there had been this well-
turned-out young guy sitting waiting to see the consul, and damned
if he hadn't his own club tie on. So Bingham said he'd stopped in
front of him and said wasn't that a Quad tie he was wearing? and the
guy'd looked up surprised and said well *yes*. So he'd said well be
damned, what class was he? and he'd said '77, what was *he*? and
he'd said '73. And the guy'd said for God's sweet sake fancy meeting
him in *this* assembly-line, what was *he* here after? So naturally he'd
said he worked here, what could he expedite for him? and it had
turned out what he wanted was some advice on apartment hunting.
Which was God's personalized service if ever there'd been—Morgan
Guaranty were just transferring his current roommate to London. So,
Bingham said, he and Chad had had lunch together, *very* agreeably,
and he'd shown him the Avenue Bosquet set-up, and when the
roommate moved out Chad had moved in.

Perfect relationship ever since. Minded his own business; also
they had a nice selection of random tastes in common. Even found
they had some of the same friends. Couple of cocks on a blue-chip
midden, yes, but the midden was of course all Western Europe.

But Ms. Godfrey seemed unappeased. Because merely how was
she to *face* the abashing man the next time she saw him? she fretted.
Because this girl— The things one learned, goodness!

He said, amused, well it was a generation she was a good many
years nearer to than alas he was. In his day girls had done their
overseas marauding on junior-year-abroad, or on fulbrights. But this
Barretts child it seemed was doing spectacularly well on her own.

Talented musically but in fact also paying her way with it, composing that bogus-Black stuff for a French nightclub band. Played piano in this band's cellar it appeared some nights herself—'the sort of enterprise our international trade balance could use a lot more of,' Bingham had put it.

—But otherwise, Sather went on, he'd pretty much drawn a blank in the Avenue Bosquet. Chad was 'somewhere in the South of France'; he rang up every now and then to ask about mail or the like; last time, he'd said he'd thought of dropping in on his married sister (who was it seemed staying with a man named Waymarsh, in Grasse); be heading home in a few days. Or probably. Or perhaps. And in short about all he'd got from his visit was that unlisted telephone number.

Ms. Godfrey said '... staying with'?

Newman family lawyer. Though what of all people Waymarsh was doing in foreign parts, God knew. Hardly part of his own operation anyhow—he doubted if Waymarsh would be even Mrs. Newman's notion of a fall-back position! And in any case that wouldn't explain what Chad's sister was doing there. What was she looking amused about?

'Overseas marauding' was *his* phrase not hers. But now with the sister too?

He said blandly well no, hardly occur to anybody to think of Waymarsh as dirty-old-man enough. Still, who knew who knew. But to go back to the Avenue Bosquet (how'd they ever got off onto something like Waymarsh good god)—the upshot was, here he now found himself, and in particular might he say *her*, with an unexpected amount of time to kill. From her point of view this might simply— Look, he said, with nothing actually to *do* but wait around until Chad turned up, marking time he meant could well be something her agency didn't—

But this was what they *did!* she cried, what did he suppose?

All the same he felt, well, diffident. So he hoped she would consider— It wasn't as if she'd have to be with him all that constantly, just that he—

But she didn't have to be 'kept amused'! When she liked him?— *and* being with him!

So he mumbled well very kind, *very* kind.

And anyway wasn't he really rather used to it, with women?

He said (and it might have been warily) oh nonsense—simply he'd found women were—how should he put it?—*nicer* to older men. They thought they were sweet or some such adjective. Or at any rate they didn't seem to feel they had to brace themselves to beat off those immediate attacks. The trouble though was it seemed to take a man all those years to find out enough of what a woman was like to treat her the way she baffled him by wanting him to, damn' sad.

Yes she said so stupid. But then if women didn't keep men's morale up somehow in the endless meantime look what they had on their hands, she said. No but to go back, had he found out what Mr. Newman occupied his time with? or was it architecture again. Or still.

Well *this* part, he said, was hardly believable. Certainly to *his* astonishment anyway, but it appeared Chad had been seriously in the stock market from by god college on! During Carter days he'd even done so well with short positions that he'd made a great deal of money. To top it off, on the election he'd not so much bet on national gullibility as plunged—and of course made a killing. A *serious* market-analyst in short! Maybe he ought to offer him a job in his own office—detach him *that* way from whoever-she-was, why not!

But then they were coming into Versailles.

And this hotel, she explained, she particularly wanted him to see, they'd have lunch there and he'd see, because it was not only Edwardian-elegant but they what used to be called 'cossetted' you. So it would be far more she thought his sort of place than that new rich-American'd one he was in, even if the Empress Eugénie *had* lived there staring sadly out over the Tuileries after she was deposed, she'd died in 1920 anyway, anyway if you were nearly a hundred did you *notice?* But *this* hotel was right at the edge of the Trianon side of the immense palace gardens, at the Porte de la Reine, in fact it was in a sort of woodsy arboretum and rose gardens of its own.

And the thing about the great hotels of the Edwardian era was how much more they were laid out for the comforts of life architecturally. In this one for instance what led to the dining room was a very long room made wide enough for tea-tables and easy chairs and love-seats, it was like an English 'long gallery,' they served tea there in winter, and all along one side of it tall French windows opened out in summer for tea or drinks onto a great terrace toward the trees, and on its inner side there was an absolutely charming white-and-gold-panelled ballroom, of course there were no balls now except at weddings, but on weekends they'd been experimenting with it as a nightclub (after of course sound-proofing the ceiling!) did he like to dance? and off it there was a little bar.

Then at the far end was the dining room and it had its terrasse outside too, toward the rose gardens, for dinner by lamplight or candles in the warm night, in high summer. And today being Sunday they had an immense buffet 'brunch,' usually sixty or seventy first-course dishes, you took a plate and served yourself, and while it was not attitudinized or *haute* cuisine it was always impeccable.

The British upper-executive class seemed to have discovered it but, still, it was a *good* hotel. And it was only ten minutes' walk from her apartment, so if he wanted to see some of France as well as

Paris while he waited for Chad to rescue his sister or whatever he was doing, it would save a *lot* of time and energy if he stayed here, he could try the buffet and look at the place and decide.

So he made a first course (which she translated dish by dish as he took some) of escabèche de poissons, fougères à la grecque, jambon persillé, langoustines, salade de riz, salade de concombres aux moules, and an artichaut farci. During which, among other things, she said if they were going to spend time together in this pleasant dallying way till Mr. Newman turned up who knew really when, shouldn't they be sensible about first names.

$$\infty$$

So next morning she moved him out to Versailles. And saw him settled in.

And then checked off at least seeing Chartres, lunch and the cathedral, where they found themselves caught up in a gaping British charabanc-tour who were being told, window by window, the plots in the stained glass.

Then back in Versailles she said voilà, and now for the evening? should she pick him up about eight for dinner? They could drive into Paris, she'd reserve a table at one of her favorite best places, it was out the Avenue du Maine and one never saw anybody there but impeccable bourgeois doing themselves *extremely* well. Also this man had a rosé d'Arbois which would be new to him, because it didn't travel—and he needn't look skeptical, it wasn't a Midi rosé it was almost a deep ruby. Arbois was in the Jura. Which is off there between Burgundy and Switzerland. It was, did he know? Pasteur's pays. But the *famous* Arbois wine was a yellow, called vin de paille: it was for dessert, like sauternes and those German trockenbeeren wines. She *had* heard they made coq au vin with it locally, but wouldn't he be dubious too?

—It however turned out that with eventually a guinea they had a Beaune; and (eyes smiling at him across the candlelight) she was inquiring gently into his character.

"Are you sort of what I'm beginning to think you are?" she asked, in a voice of almost promises, "—or more anyway Lewis I mean than I thought you were, sort of, at first?"

He said oh he was pretty much standard fare. Made money. Spent it. Made more. Tended to spend that then too.

"No but I meant your—how you *live* generally, do with your time and all I mean."

If she meant his spare time, he had a sloop in the Sound. And played squash winters. But if she meant was he married, no he wasn't. Had been, years ago. Charming girl too. Got tired of each other, of course. Amicably tired, but tired. She'd remarried. Hadn't seen her for years. Amicably tired of his successor too by this time very likely. Restless like anyone.

"But you," she persisted, "you're 'sophisticated' the way Americans are sophisticated when they are. I do like the way you look, Lewis, shall I alarm you by saying? But do you think, possibly, you might be happier if you were sophisticated the way Europeans are? Or think they are—having had their parochial worries longer."

He said, smiling, oh now now. He made do.

"Yes but I mean your character, Lewis, are you perhaps a little, well, melancholy?" she asked, as if in tender amusement. "Should I try to divert you specially somehow?—take you to the Grand Véfour say in my yellow silk? that one of the girls at Chanel (they *all* do, you know) copied for me absolutely stitch for stitch, because how am I to know about you? You make it sound so bleak, 'make do.'"

Well she was sweet, he said; but of course it never struck you as bleak at the time, how could it? One picked up a lovely signal, if that was what she was asking. At a party. Across a milling room. The signals he supposed differed from generation to generation, but suddenly a look would say—and to *you*—'Here I am. . . .' A pretty woman was bored with her husband. Or disillusioned with a lover. Likely of course to be the fellow's own damn' fault. But suppose at the moment one had too much unprincipled indolence to refuse. It could even last the whole season. Then off for the summer, Maine or the Cape or wherever, and by autumn each of you would have gone on, even if a bit apologetically, to something new. A bit of nostalgia and tenderness first time you met again, but that was simply good manners. Did he need to describe it? Been divorced herself hadn't she?

She was silent.

Well but hadn't she?

So she murmured, ". . . differently," smiling a little.

Well, however it was. Simply there was this disenchantment, was the principle. How did women operate either? So it was targets of opportunity. He'd had a wicked old uncle who as good as reduced it to a formula—'Absolute dish of a girl. Married, too, which is always convenient.'

" 'Convenient'!"

Well, he'd admit, yes, it did sound a bit lazy—competition only a husband. Who'd have lost her already presumably—otherwise this lovely thunderbolt wouldn't be poised over your head. No, but his uncle had an entirely humane position even if he didn't put it that way. And even if it looked like a dilemma of egotism! Because what kind of (it might be) desperation *was* it standing there looking her question straight at you? How did you know you weren't being asked for an act of humanity?—being *trusted* for it!

"Oh but *Lewis*," she said, laughing at him, "you can't be saying you think of your sexual behavior as high-minded!"

Plato thought *his* was didn't he? No, be serious—suppose you're her first. She's nerved herself up to something she may even have been brought up to be shocked at. And the *risk* she's running! Is a decent-minded man to back irresponsibly off? And leave a perhaps very sweet woman to some eventual oaf who'll do no better by her than her husband? Hadn't she *seen* what some of her clients were like?

"Are you?" she said lightly, watching the waiter serve their feuilleté aux framboises.

Ah he and they were all pretty much of an age and kind, he said, watching too. Next year his class would have their thirtieth reunion. She know what most of them would turn up thinking?—even saying? 'Well I'm still by god alive anyway!' She conceive of it? Man after man of them! Appalling! Well then what kind of husband was that to stay appetizingly faithful to. Hadn't done what, thirty years before, they'd confidently expected. Or hoped. Hadn't had a respectable number of love affairs. Didn't even seem to be aware they hadn't. Hadn't of course paid enough elementary attention to women to *have* had. Hardly any longer try—poor sods given that up too. Whereas all these goddam young men (they'll complain to you) mind you in *our own college*— All right, he said, giggle, but most of them were a breed that hadn't really *understood* anything much that happens to the race of man since they were told in kindergarten it didn't, and he found it *sad!*

"No but Lewis what I was ask—"

Made all kinds of money, yes, but then what? Just morosely make more? Make enough to parlay it up dear god into Washington? Would she believe that a couple of bankery dull bastards he was at Yale with were now *making* foreign policy, God help us all? ...

So she teased him. "Are you perhaps just a *little* an intellectual snob? No but Lewis to go back I mean—you can't always just stand there looking humane and available till somebody comes up and says 'Console me' can you, or shouldn't I ask?"

Laugh if she liked, he said amiably, but what could anybody do, considering the reciprocating incompetences? The expectations, the hair-raising myths, one grew up in! . . . For instance the sense in which one was or was not somebody's property was beyond a layman to define. 'Tenancy at will' perhaps a lawyer would call it—but then, at the end of it, were you entitled to emblements or weren't you?

"But Lewis where would men be," she protested, teasing still, "if every now and then a woman didn't make a totally incompetent decision about you?"

Thank God of *course*. But suppose it was God forbid an old friend's wife who'd suddenly looked her immemorial query into your eyes—in that *instant* what black gulfs of revelation had opened! And this, mind you, about a man you'd known perhaps from prep-school on, and assumed was as like you in attitudes as another man could be. And no doubt was. But now?—how many secret hours had she been considering you, wondering about you, weighing you, *comparing* you, and now *this* difference! And if you answered that lovely look, think before the night was out what you would have been pitilessly told, and listened to as comfortless for him as she. He conceded, the consensus was it was comedy. As his old uncle used to say, 'Why *not* seduce a friend's wife?—far more humane than causing pain to some poor chap you hardly know.' But his uncle had never been anything but a bachelor. So did she see?

"And you don't call *that* bleak?" she cried.

Let him finish, dammit. All this was just the, well, the scenario one seemed to be handed. But the theme, for him, was the actors rather than the action. Or call it style. The beginnings of an affair were of course in themselves a great pleasure. But they were hardly the end a man of experience would have in mind. Who anybody *was* was the final charming secret; and this, the girl in your arms might only decide to let you think you were discovering. Though even for that she had to be convinced you really wanted to know. For all he could tell, the ultimate humanity was *not* finding it out anyhow—the history of Western civilization had been its processes, after all, not our endlessly mistaken 'answers.' Put another way, he said, smiling at her, was there anyone to talk to to your heart's content but someone in your arms?

"But oh *dear!*" she cried. "But Lewis how *wicked* and disarming! Are you really as—"

'Disarming'!—when it was merely how he did see it? good god there'd been times when he felt like Lord Chesterfield, 'the most agreeable things he had ever heard had been from persons in a horizontal position.'

So she looked at him smiling.

But she said, "No but how am I to describe it to anyone who hasn't *been* besieged? your way or not. You all say why *not* fall in love, what good does it do not to?—as if that were the argument! When really there isn't any argument, is there. Because nothing a man says is plausible, it's *he* who is. Or, most of the time, isn't, poor sweet."

He said what kind of heartless stodgy word was this 'besiege' of hers! No man laid siege, in any case, the way she meant it. It was women made these lovely decisions wasn't it? so all a 'siege' was was a man's modest signal that he hoped he might be decided on, and knew he sometimes was.

And so forth and so on.

But as it was still clearly too soon for any of this theory to be put into practice, they had for that evening wordlessly left it at that.

Next morning, though, he had said yes, well, but what was *she* like then generally either? And as this trip he was driving, she could look at him carefully, though what she had the moment before been doing was fill him in on the economics and geography of the Cotentin peninsula.

For though he had said there were some things in Paris he'd like to see, the Jeu de Paume pictures for instance, after New York wasn't Paris in most ways just another great city? and France must have other countrysides rather less bland than those vistas going out to Chartres. Country was in fact what he'd like to see most. And architecture was a hobby of his, if they had time. But also his father had been in the 1944 invasion; in filial piety he ought to go look at Omaha Beach, could they do it in a day?

So they were well on their way to Caen when he asked what she was like then generally either.

"How d'you mean," she said, " 'either'?"

Meant how she happened to be, for one thing, living in France like this.

"But I love France! And the French let you breathe. I had a Tourangelle grandmother, I used to visit her in the summer. Ever since I can remember. France is *home*. So after my divorce I put ads in college alumni magazines, and *very* soon I was so busy I needed a partner. Now after three years and a half there are three of us, and extras on call. And really Lewis it is a lovely life—expense-account lovely anyway. Some clients I told you can be yearning and tiresome, but when they're good-looking and high-powered it's good for one's morale."

Then she mustn't have stayed married long.

"Oh but Lewis I told you—it was stupid. I mean I shouldn't have *married* him, it was perfectly sweet as it was. But then my roommate was having this horsing-around *messy* affair and I guess it was sort of contrast."

'Messy'?

"Yes with this professor of English. Because he had this just devastating campus reputation, among other things he gave a very advanced course in James Joyce and you had to be interviewed to get into it, and then once you were in, *then* he took his pick. Well anyway that was the myth, and girls got besotted about him. On the wall over his bed there was a needlepoint sampler one of his girls had made him as a valentine, all hearts and cowrie shells, and it had a motto from *Finnegans Wake*, 'Hadn't he seven dams to wive him each with her different hue and cry,' and he certainly did!"

He said catnip, huh.

"Well he *was*, I guess. And my roommate was a crazy girl and for a *joke* went to be interviewed. Only she came back looking sort of stunned and out of her mind, and said well she'd *heard* how he affected students 'but oh god Maria that's how he's affected *me!*' Well *hilarious* of course but don't you see also it's rather scary? to see somebody totally lose her head over a man like that? Because *instantly* you think suppose it happens to *me!*"

And sometimes he said it does.

She murmured, "... yes," as if humbly.

This Edwardian old uncle of his, he said, used to amuse himself concocting turn-of-the-century epigrams about that sort of thing. They dated, he supposed, epigrams. But he remembered one that wasn't far from the point. 'What the lovely things are up to in bed with us they seldom say. In the opinion of competent observers they seldom know.' The style was, he'd concede, dated.

"But my roommate wasn't!"

Not all that difference! Yale innocently went coed before her roommate's time didn't it? and he gathered the sudden delicious new perquisites had left the faculty exhausted.

"You don't have to snicker!" she cried. "Girls need to practice on *somebody*—and what practice does a boy give? All the *work* still to be done on him, goodness!"

He said amiably they'd let another woman do the buffing-up? Damn' lazy, if you asked him. Not to say running risks! Or had perhaps something of the sort (if she'd permit him to ask, in sympathy need he say not from curiosity)—had something like that been the trouble in her marriage?

"Oh no *that* wasn't the trouble," she said. "He was sweet. I mean I suppose he still is, he's sort of a writer."

He said he saw.

So she stared at him. "I don't see how you can 'see'!" she cried. "What could being a writer have to do with it? Oh well you might as well *know* about me I guess. Simply I fell out of love with him. But he kept on being upset, I mean after the divorce too. So once I did really give it a second try, Lewis. Because he rang up from New York. He was coming to the South of France around Easter, he was going to hole up somewhere near Le Canadel and write a novel, and *please* wouldn't I try again. If nothing else, we could stay at Nîmes or Arles and go to the bullfights, I'd be going south for Easter like everybody else wouldn't I? So I thought oh dear. But it wasn't as if I were in love then with anybody else. And, well, after all I *hadn't* you know made love for practically ages, in love or not. So I said to him well I would *try* meeting him, better perhaps in Arles, I said, we'd be less likely to run into somebody I knew than in Nîmes, which for one thing is three times as big, so all right I'd meet him, the bulls would be fun. And he sounded oh just so helplessly *happy*, all those thousands of miles of lonely ocean away, that I was *touched*, it could have been me, I suppose. So he met my plane in Marseille, and when we got to the hotel in Arles I found he'd been so uncertain, poor sweet, about how he was afraid I might feel, that he'd taken separate rooms for us, and I was touched all over again."

He said dangerous.

"Well *yes!* The most *total* self-trap! But I was so attendrie I almost wondered whether it wouldn't be kind to be a poule de luxe that night for him, the way I used to do for his birthday. And once for Christmas. Only of course *that* would have left him feeling even more bereft when I was gone. Oh dear, what are you looking like that for?—hasn't any girl ever done a Special Occasion for you?"

Hardly though in *these* particular—what should he call them?— these re-marital circumstances.

"But haven't you ever taken up again with somebody?"

He said oh a couple of times, yes.

"Like what."

Usual thing—a bit sad.

"You're ashamed of it?"

Certainly not!

"Then *tell!*"

Why, he said, it was simply for instance like a visiting girl he'd met at a rowdy party of a classmate's and he found haunted him after she'd gone home to her Berkeley husband. So, presently, on a trip to see clients he had in San Francisco, like an infatuated boy he'd rung her number. What opinion of his past behavior he'd have when he was seventy, God knew; but her voice again, answering her phone there in her house across the bay— Was it God's plan to have us unteachably susceptible, or what? The party might have been no more than the night before!

"The rowdy party?"

In one of those formal old brick houses in East Eleventh, it had been, in the Village. Normal Village party of the era, too—everybody tight in the usual pleasantly pointless way; on into the usual small hours; usual drunken bellows of goodnight echoing up the stairwell from the dark hall below as at long last it was ending; and suddenly this girl had materialized before him. As if from nowhere. Mind you he hadn't said ten words to her all evening—somebody had introduced them, hours back, and they'd said hello, and so help him not ten words since. But now here this charming thing stood, eyes looking gravely into his. It could have been a dream, it was so strange.

And taken aback he supposed he must have appeared, for she'd reached up, looking amused, and let a wrist fall lightly on each of his shoulders, as if it were a ritual—and what was he to have done. They stood there; they might have been alone in the world. Then she said softly, 'Where do you live? . . .' and that year he happened to be living just round the block, in East Tenth.

So, well, in short, when he opened his eyes in the lovely summer-Sunday dawn, she was sitting on the edge of his bed in a yellow Chinese dressing-gown of his, with the cuffs turned back from her wrists, gazing down at him with no particular expression. He had gazed back, his mind foggily reconstructing. After a minute or two he'd said, 'Thinking me over? . . .' and after a minute or two of her own she'd murmured, 'Should I?' and then there had been this slightly smiling silence. Until, finally, he'd more or less mumbled, 'I wasn't, you know, standard. . . .' and she'd given this little yelp of amusement, 'Heavens did you think *I* was?' and toppled giggling down into his arms.

Maria said, "Oh *dear*," looking at him. "Are you always being spoiled like this?"

'Spoiled'!

"Well goodness but don't you think?"

Hardly call it a thing like 'spoiled'—good god the angel had had to go home to her damn' husband before even the week was out!

"Oh *poor* man!" she mocked. "So deserted so forlorn! How could *any* woman!"

Ah, well, he said, amusing wasn't how you saw these things at the time. When you'd been stunned? When there wasn't world enough and time for the feast you were being deprived of? He'd seen her off at Newark as good as wordless with woe. She too: at the end she'd just managed a last choking '. . . Take care of yourself?' and fled down the tunnel to her plane. Without a glance back. And he had turned and come away, death in his soul.

So Maria looked at him solemnly, as respecting this.

Dismal he said in fact all round. And then, would she believe it? in San Francisco she'd, she'd tearfully refused even to see him.

"Oh Lewis how *awful!*"

Been fairly bad, yes. Though likely enough would've been bad seeing her too. Who was to say.

"But why?"

How'd anyone know. Probably been a great mistake to give her time to come to her senses. Or at least decide whether he was worth the, call it the turmoil, the emotional risks. In fact she'd said so— 'Oh sweet do you really want us to have to get over each other a *second* time? . . .' He found he remembered every accusing syllable. In short she'd been sensible: a damn' shame. Though he supposed how not. Heart-breaking, though, if you liked stately terms. But one had to expect it—women had somehow edited the sensibilities-scenario so it was always they who were nobly wounded. Which he presumed was what conferred on them the right to say Yes or No. It had been she, hadn't it? who'd agreed to meet this ex-husband of hers again! And had the poor devil dared more than take a separate room for her like a gent?

"Oh Lewis don't be tiresome—what was I down there *for*, heavens!"

... But he thought hadn't she said she was touched?

"But who wouldn't be? He was sweet. But being touched isn't falling in love, heavens. And how could any man think being unassuming was a way to put me in a swoon about him—well, one despairs! And then oh it was so perfectly *silly*—couldn't I always have said No to him in the same room? But then if I was going to decide to make love with him again, why pay for an extra room! And anyway what on earth did he imagine the patronne thought a man and a girl came to her hotel in the Easter vacation to *do* besides eat and go to bullfights!—so he'd made us look childishly innocent of the world as *well* as perfectly ridiculous. I never did find out who he gave her to understand I was—for all I know he told her I was an old friend or something, and of course what 'une ancienne amie' *means*, poor dear, is 'a former mistress.' When why explain at all! Well naturally the patronne's manners were impeccable, this is after all France, but imagine arriving to find oneself stuck with such a hopeless méprise! And when *anybody* in the hotel could see he was all blissful over me, so the separate bedrooms looked sillier still!"

Hard to bear, Sather said; um.

"And then he didn't know every hotel in Arles is booked *weeks* ahead for the bullfights—so after two days the patronne was terribly sorry for Monsieur's malentendu but we must vacate our rooms! We were appalled; we said but what were we to *do*, go back to Paris at *Easter?*—surely she could find us a room somewhere! She said well she did have a cousin who had an attic apartment that might not be taken, but Madame and Monsieur—well, there were two *beds* in her cousin's grenier, but it was just the one room, if Madame understood ... ? So I thought very fast and said but had she or perhaps her cousin by any chance a paravent? because something like that, didn't she think, between the beds . . . So of course instantly she was beaming and d'accord, *much* relieved, mais bien sûr she had a paravent if in effect that would turn the difficulty for Madame, she would send a girl at once to her cousin's to make sure the apartment was still free. I saw I said no difficulties whatever, Monsieur and I were perfectly débrouillards and in any case we had known each other since childhood; and off she went. He said 'What in God's name's a paravent?' I said a folding screen, what did he think. He said, 'She thinks a *screen*'s going to preserve your modesty?' I said, 'Heavens d'you think she believes we were childhood friends either? Just this is good manners and *France*.' So, presently, there was this solemn little procession up through the streets to her cousin's attic—us, two maids with our luggage, and a little old man from the cousin's pottering along behind with the paravent. I thought it was *hilarious!*" she finished.

Husband, though, probably didn't?

"No he did too. But then after the bullfights I anyway transplanted us off to Aix—to *one* room, and if he behaved like an undergraduate, what matter."

So for a kilometer or so they were silent.

Presently she said, "But then anyway it turned out I wasn't any wilder about him than before. So it didn't work out."

Ah well, he said, she'd been a sweet to try.

"But now he's written a very dejected novel about it. It isn't published yet, but he sent me a copy of the manuscript. It's sort of what the French called Nouveau Roman, only of course that's been out-of-date for twenty years, d'you suppose he didn't know? Anyway, *his* is written in what you called stately terms, not French at all."

He said, sounding amused, 'wild about'?—what kind of criterion was that!

"Well isn't it?" she demanded. "You needn't sound sardonic and superior! Haven't you ever lost your head? Or do you just go round being hard to get over!"

Writing a novel about a sad parting with a girl you'd not been able to forget, he said smoothly, hardly struck him as a sensible way to forget her. Though ah, who was sensible. Some heavenly creature took your breath away by walking into your arms—only to change her damn' mind about you and walk out of them with just as little explanation. Enough for any man to hang himself over. Particularly when young. And she, Maria, might he add—well, after these four days of her he didn't wonder at the depths the poor devil's dejection must have plunged him to! Could ruin any novel, what'd she expect! She know that mock-Restoration lyric?—

> Why should a decent-minded God
> Trouble my sleep with you?

—that wasn't a question, God *bless* no, that was a complaint to the Management.

So for a long moment she gazed at him so soberly that she nearly let him miss the turn-off for Dives-Cabourg.

Where, then, before the estuary, they stopped at a charcuterie for pâté de campagne and saucisson sec, at a bakery for a baguette, and at a Suma for a wedge of Brie, three hundred grammes of Breton strawberries, a bottle of Brouilly, and a packet of paper napkins.

Next morning she rang him at breakfast to ask what should she propose they do today? assuming Jock Bingham had still no word from Chad. Perhaps *not* so far as Normandy this time? Would he like to see Rambouillet?—the château and the lovely forest? They could set out late-morning, it wasn't far, and eat somewhere on the way. At Le Perray there was a charming inn, set in what the French called a parc. Or, a little off the direct route, a *very* good restaurant at Châteaufort. So they could be back for tea, the hotel served beautiful pastry, he could have a tarte aux fraises des bois, and he could phone Mrs. Newman, wasn't six o'clock here midmorning there?

He said fine, fine; if she meant a lazy day, why not; end up perhaps with dinner at the hotel and then go dancing there, she care to? he hadn't brought evening clothes but *she* could dress, to dazzle him.

—And dazzling in fact she was, in half-naked summer black, and they had dinner, late, out on the rose-garden terrasse in the soft June evening, the myriad gleam of candles from table to table so barely luminous a dusk there were aisles as of outer darkness between, each table might have been a little tent of light pitched secret and apart, lit from within, so that women's eyes shone like dark gold in it for you, lustrous and a marvel, or with a glitter as of promise no matter what in their minds lay hidden and unguessed. At a table near, a man Sather's age perhaps and a young woman of Maria's were surely (Maria murmured) in love—it was how they gazed, and twice she said the girl's fingertips had touched his hand. Except but oh *look*, had she brought her *children* to a rendezvous?—for on a dusky balcony two stories above two small girls in summer nightgowns were peering over the railing down, and presently, giggling with love, they'd begun dropping crumbs (from their suppers?) down onto that table, and soon the whole terrasse was sharing in the amusement.

Sather said 'lovers'? nonsense. The fellow was much too old. Must be her father. Or uncle.

" 'Too old'—with *your* history?" she teased. "Hoh!"

What history.

"Well you might admit for once mightn't you? I mean for instance look, you've had affairs with girls *ten* years younger than you haven't you?—well, so then have you with a girl fifteen years younger ever too?"

So naturally he snorted at her. What was this sociological Socratic elenchus leading up to—the difference in ages (alas) between the two of *them?*

She said sweetly, "Well or shouldn't it? No but I mean Lewis for instance that Berkeley girl you seem to've so completely— And if you didn't want me to ask questions about her you shouldn't have boasted! So how much was *she* younger?"

Damned if he'd boasted! He'd merely—

"Fifteen years younger? *Twenty?*"

How was he to know?—hardly the sort of thing you asked! Could have been anything more or less young. What did age have to do with it anyhow.

So she looked at him it seemed astonished.

"But Lewis didn't you even think what she could have been *through* over you?" she demanded. "Because I mean at that age meeting an attractive man who can help thinking 'oh what would it be like to have him?' only then there is the danger too, you *know* how fast you fall in love—so all evening long she could have been in this fever or spellbound or seduced or whatever. *But waiting.* For what if you were working your way toward her through the party uproar. Only what if she turned round and you weren't. Or weren't even near. Or were leaving . . . And then abruptly there was the party beginning to break up, with *nothing* decided about you, she hadn't even shut her eyes and wished; and she simply— Well what would anybody do! she came up to you in this daze and just helplessly claimed you, do you understand *anything?*" she more or less accused him.

So (if only courteously to the contrary) he was silent.

"Oh well I know not 'claimed,'" she fretted, "but it was a choice wasn't it? I mean, *serious!* Not just a have-bed-will-bundle. Or as if you'd been just anybody. And then next morning a choice all over again, and certainly *then* réfléchi. So I don't see how she could just go back to her life or whatever. Or even why did you let her!" she cried, as if past belief.

—Later, though, as if continuing, and this was hours later, the shadowy white and gold of the ballroom as if softly candle-lit too for the slow wheeling patterns of the dancers—turning and turning in his arms to the music's discourse she murmured, ". . . or did you I guess have your usual New York girl you were being unfaithful to then too?" so gently she might, already, have had a right to indulge him.

So, as such things go, a good deal of what may nevertheless want saying could be considered said.

The rest of the ritual following naturally dans les formes too. "Because what I seem to be trying you know to make up my mind about," she told him, as they turned, "is *are* you more what I wondered whether you mightn't turn out to be than I'd expected I'd think."

He said (amused, having decoded this) why, he hoped an attitude of the most respectful attentiveness—

"Oh Lewis *don't* be bogus-worldly at me!" she begged. "Because but anyway no, what I mean is, somehow we've— It does seem I've— *Have* you taken a fancy to me?"

When she'd dammit explicitly warned him *off?!*

"But sweet that was only—"

And before they'd good god more than sat down at Drouant! In the face of *that* charming No—and at his age!—was he to have presumed on what an absolute darling to be with he'd found her, to insist on telling her how adorable he found her too?

"You're not perhaps just softening my heart Lewis in the usual low male way?"

He said, smiling, dammit he was a modest man! Why was he to think the happy details of how he felt about her weren't exactly what she'd forbidden him to recite?

"But goodness," she said, smiling too, "is it something to sound so sad about? All the average man requires is the services of a small portable woman of some kind. But you aren't *that* average are you? Should I reflect about you I mean d'you think?" she ended, teasing.

So it became merely a question of which of them shouldn't too abruptly suggest wasn't it perhaps time (tomorrow's excursion starting early)—time they called it an evening? and he saw her home? it being, after all, by then, well on into the small hours anyway.

Though she did murmur a gently tactical "Ah do I really fetch you Lewis?—and so soon?" slipping a hand through his arm as they sauntered off through the hotel gates into the summer night of the Avenue de la Reine and along under the lindens in the dark, the gleam of a street lamp only here and there sifting down through the dusty foliage into patterns of leaf-shadow across the cracks and crevices of the pavement. And when at the carrefour they turned into her Avenue du Roi, silent and fathomless it too among its looming shadows, "*Are* you hard to get over?" she asked—but teasing still, so he could answer (as why not?) well he tried his gentlemanly damn' best to be! and in a happy voice she could pretend, "But suppose the lovely roof fell in on us . . ." until under the lamp at the corner of her cross street they wandered to a stop and kissed, lightly, tastingly, a good dozen times it could have been, before drifting murmuring on.

So at last, at her door in the black starlight, she said almost dreamily, ". . . and when you've never even seen me home before, oh sweet isn't it strange," rummaging in her handbag for her key. "And then *this*," she mumbled, and slotted the key into the lock.

—Hours, then, it may have been, later (dawn, outside, if they'd bothered to look) that she seemed to decide, for whatever reason, to set at least part of the ambiguities drowsily straight.

". . . It was my other partner, you know, not me."

He made some vague dozing sound.

"Who had I mean an affair with Jock Bingham."

Did, huh, he agreed; *well*.

"And still maybe *is* having was why I sounded I guess startled that day."

. . . 'd wondered, yes.

"Because you *aren't* are you sweetie going to be stupid and jealous over me?"

He said no.

∞

They slept late.

—And slept late the second morning too, for that matter.

But then in due course later still ("Le petit déjeuner. De mon amant. Est sur la table. Mon amour get *up*, I am teaching you aren't-you-hungry French") dawdling over breakfast too in the brilliance and happy senses of on toward noon (" 'Complacencies of the peignoir' oh sweet 'and late coffee and oranges,' well it's a sortie de bain of course not a peignoir, but 'par complaisance' oh *dear!*") she began the reconstruction of their history, myths and all.

"Tell me something? I mean the *truth*?"

So he looked amused and wary.

"Did you feel I was a *long* time making up my mind about you? Or did you."

"I was to have expected *this?*" he demanded, sounding courteously astonished.

"Oh sweet but sort of weren't you?"

"When the first thing you did was recite your agency's virginal damn' ground-rules at me?"

"As if *you* were in the habit of just letting girls say No to you!" she grieved. "Hoh!"

He said agreeably, "Properly brought up, is all. Did as I thought I was being told. Thought I was supposed to."

"Hoh!"

"Look, my angel," he said, as if explaining, "how could any man in his right mind—"

"Well but *was* I? Longer? Than your usual girls!"

There being no such thing as a usual girl, what was a reasonable man to say?

So he declaimed (and in fact reasonably). For quite aside, dammit, from the sheer bad manners of disbelieving her to her face, how could any man in his dazzled senses have had the, the effrontery to assume anything as lovely as *she* was wasn't already—if she'd forgive him the stuffiness of an archaism—already spoken for!

"But Lewis all I told you—"

He said be quiet. Because quite simply— Look, would she have the womanly candor to admit? simply she was a beauty, and against beauty what could a man do? It stunned you, it transfixed you. In a word, for him anyhow (he said rhetorically), it was as daunting as death, and damn' well by now she must know it, he ended, waiting to be smiled at.

So at least she looked at him more reasonably.

And conceded, "I don't really I suppose want to hear about your other girls anyway do I."

He said *god* no.

"No, but about you," she now said, as if in a kind of tender and anxious cherishing, "ah Lewis have you had so *little* pleasure in your life? 'Making do.' *Shall* I take you to the Grand Véfour in full fig and cheer you up, poor sweet? and I mean see?"

Well he said she was a blessing, but what kind of dotty methodology was this?—she been making love with him just to 'cheer him up'?!

"Ah, Lewis," she said, sounding hurt, "can't I worry a little about you besides other things? I never had an affair with a disabused man. Of course I don't mean that was *why*. But you *are* a little melancholy, Lewis. And I started asking myself why you were, I suppose. And was curious about you. And sorry. And I remember one day we were driving—this must have been that second day?— we were anyway driving and suddenly I thought But I'm looking at him differently, heavens does my face show it? and I said to you, 'I'm beginning to think you're not solemn at all.' "

So he mildly snorted.

"And d'you remember what you said? you said, 'Then you might even stop being daughterly to me!'—which you will admit was, well, *was!* because oh dear I realized *that* wasn't how I felt like being to you, and I looked at you in a sort of terror—I mean there you were, experienced and charming and unknowable, how would I ever expect to know how many girls had loved you? And all this so *sudden*, Lewis, like one's doom. So see?" she said happily. "So now I do find myself being a little mad about you, temporarily!"

'Temporarily!'

"Well isn't it?"

This, any more in passing for her than—

"Oh Lewis, do I have to remind you how the dialogue always goes?—this is *comedy!* You say in this romantic voice, sounding just irresistible, 'I don't want to leave ever,' and I absolutely melt inside and say, 'Oh sweet I don't ever want you to,' but does that mean either of us thinks you're going to stay? And sweetie you do rather, well, have a history of living off the country don't you?"

But dammit he said do a man and a woman just any day find themselves in *this* sort of miraculous—

"Oh but that's what I *mean*," she mourned. "Because I don't think I know how to deal with it!—I mean have I lost my head over you like a schoolgirl or do you just so totally please me? Or is *that* losing one's head! And you don't even seem to realize I shouldn't be *asking* such a question, even, this soon!" she reproached him, as if who could not. "Didn't you *see* I was falling in love with you?"

He said but—

"But when so many girls have been in love with you it isn't *possible* you didn't know!"

He said in the first place dammit there hadn't been all that many. And in the second, how was he to have been sure that 'agency policy' of hers was anything but a well-brought-up young woman's way of reminding a man of fifty that fifty, alas, was pretty much the age her father was, champagne to start with or no champagne.

And anyhow, he said, amiably, if he might say so, women's 'falling in love,' as a trope, had often seemed to him to be not so much a passion per se as a way of behaving, a part of the good manners of being a woman. A style; a procedure, even. Of course it was a pastime too—Restoration comedy for instance wasn't even about anything much else, and there were still, God knows— Well, wasn't it a matter of amour propre?—if you weren't in love what was wrong with you!

She said, "You discuss us as if we were some sort of natural phenomenon."

"Ah well," he said, "but aren't you?"

"Oh Lewis of course who now and then doesn't," she admitted.

"Because it is silly not to make love now and *then* with somebody nice. One doesn't have to be 'in love' dans les formes—heavens, do men? After my divorce I was dancing once at this party in somebody's studio and he was very nice, and that lovely electricity began flickering. You know? But then I thought oh but this is just what women *do* after a divorce, oh *damn!*—and anyhow I was just back in Paris again and *much* too busy starting my agency. To I mean fall in *love*."

Some Frenchman this was?

"Oh no he wasn't French, I wasn't *that* light-minded, no he was this very nice— Oh well if you'd really like to know it was Jock Bingham," she said, as if abashed. "But I didn't have an affair with him—it was my partner was why I was startled about your Barretts girl. Because Lewis I did have to concentrate on starting my agency. I'd had the idea of it long before the divorce, you know, but commuting, sort of, instead, between New York and France."

That perhaps had something to do with the divorce?

"Oh well that wasn't the real trouble. With our marriage, that is. *That* was, that I fell in love with somebody else. But he did love me, Lewis, I mean my husband. His whole novel's about me, in Arles. About what he calls 'the feast' of me. It made me feel like a Matisse odalisque, goodness! You can read it if you like."

He said oh well, very kind, thank 'ee yes. 'Feast' was a lovely word for her, her husband was a man of talent; why didn't she come round *this* side of the breakfast table?

So when presently she'd fetched the manuscript she did. And perched on his knee so he could read around her in comfort.

Then here I am, without her.

No longer sure who I am, without her. A man lacking routine identity. A man very possibly unrecognizable.

His identity now in an airport bus en route to Marignane; en route to her plane to Rome.

A man, simply, in a daze.

Sather said, "What were you doing in Rome?"

"But visiting my dear mother, pet. She lives in Rome, part of the year. She loves it."

"This thing have a title?"

"He's still deciding on one. He wanted to call it 'Maria As An Art Form,' but I said how silly."

A man, simply, in a daze.

Though no doubt in appearance a normally definable (tall; dazed) pedestrian descending, among other pedestrians descending/ascending, these flights of broad stone stair, these gardens; in a city he would a fortnight ago have spelled (with a non-existent S) Marseilles; proceeding moreover to a definable destination (a Quai des Belges); the data including in particular what the briefest of inquiries would establish, viz., a man perdutamente innamorato, a man violently in love, and now of no more identity than merely that.

Wasn't this all kind of mannered?

"But Lewis I told you! He's being stylistically Nouveau Roman. Of course in an end-of-the-fifties way. But maybe he's parodying somebody French."

No longer a man who this now vanished fortnight ago had met her plane from Orly; no longer even a man in whose arms only this far-off morning she had woken murmuring, to indulge with sleepy love.

"So Maria was an art form then too?"

She nuzzled him, giggling.

Except then "Oh maybe I shouldn't I suppose have met him again poor sweet at all, or d'you think," she admitted. "Oh dear am I hard to get over too?"

He said god *yes* she'd be!

"I didn't mean for *you*."

No but look dammit, he said, this poor devil—meeting her again was a headlong folly, yes, the odds totally God knew against him, but he *felt* for this ex-husband of hers, helpless or not!—hadn't she *any* idea what a heart-stopping thing she'd be to have lost? So would she mind if they didn't read any more of the thing. The poor guy shouldn't of course have put it on paper if he'd object, but all the same— *Really* she oughtn't to go round reducing men to states like that, over-articulate or not! Himself he hoped included.

But "*You*, my darling," she said forgivingly, "aren't likely to be infatuated with anybody ever. So don't *fuss*," she ended; and in due course they went into Paris for lunch, and afterwards to the Jeu de Paume.

And after that, window-shopping in the Rue du Bac, he bought her a pair of antique gold ear-rings, apparently Directoire.

∽

So if it had turned out that they were waiting *this* contentedly for young Newman (Sather said next morning at breakfast) mightn't they even have time for some architecture, for instance how far off were the Loire châteaux?—anyway wasn't that where she'd grown up spending summers at her French grandmother's?

But imagine his remembering! yes she was practically du pays, she was even told she had a Touraine accent. Actually her grandmother lived on a tributary, the Indre; at a little place called

Veigné. But *yes,* in three days they could have a wonderful trip! And eat *very* well, there was a splendid variety of river-fishes— salmon, pike, perch, and did he like eel? The regional sauces did tend to be mostly crayfish'd, when they weren't beurre blanc, but would he complain? They could spend the first night at Luynes, say, and have a *perfect* regional dinner of mousseline de brochet aux queues d'écrevisses!

But *not,* though, did he mind, visit her grandmother. ("She's much too French—if *we* dropped in, sweetie, she'd think I loved you or something. . . .")

So they decided, and he went back to the hotel to pack.

—Where however the concierge had a message for him: a Mr. Bingham had telephoned, and would Monsieur, at his earliest convenience, have the kindness to ring him back.

And when he did (he told Maria in due course) Bingham reported Chad *was* finally it appeared on his way. The damn' boy'd called in last night, from Annecy, in the Haute Savoie. Which the hotel concierge informed him was 547 kilometers from Paris, 'an easy day's drive.' So that dammit was that; and in the end she just took him to a restaurant in the Rue Le Peletier which did Loire specialties, where they dutifully discussed the prospects.

"Of course you're a sweet to say I've 'made your mission irrelevant,' " Maria said, "but specifically, Lewis, what are you going to do when Mr. Newman's back—argue with him?"

He said god no. Just more or less open-mindedly present the case for the boy's going reasonably home. The financial case. Which was all it was. Then up to him to decide.

"But what about his girl? Or haven't you thought about her. I suppose she's with him. I wonder what she *is* like."

Could be anything. Including couldn't-be-nicer.

"Are you going to see her d'you think too?"

Not really much point, was there?

"But Lewis suppose she's in love with him. In her place I'd be *outraged* at you—coming to piggishly break everything up! And just for his awful mother!"

But why assume a break-up? God help him would any young man in his right mind, Princetonian or not, want to spend the rest of his days in a couplings-empire in Iowa? Or consider the contrary. Suppose the girl was beginning to be tired of the fellow anyway— what a blessing to her *he*'d be! How nobly and for Chad's own good she could be rid of him! Because they had no idea when this affair mightn't have begun had they? And in any case, what *was* a median duration for enchantment!

"But then what did Mrs. Newman expect you to do?"

So he began to laugh. The discussion with Mrs. Newman, he said, had revolved around the size of the probable expense....

"Oh Lewis *no!*"

He *swore* it!

"But how could any woman think like that!—in *1983?*"

Time-lag would hardly affect a thing like maternal jealousy! Lucky thing perhaps, on the whole, that Chad had made money of his own. Though of course who could tell, it even *might* turn out he'd opt for the factories.

So they decided there was nothing, actually, for them to decide.

And so why not window-shop, she said, through the Sixième Arrondissement, how many friends did he want to buy presents for? Including for secretaries? And they could end up for tea at the Closerie des Lilas, simply enjoying themselves.

At the Closerie however, things being as they are, it turned out she went on with her inquiry into his life and loves.

"Were they all people's wives?"

"Dear god, Maria," he said, "what's natural selection!"

"You mean we all just fall into your arms like me?" she said. "Don't you ever go *after* people?"

"Went after you!"

"You didn't, you just *behaved*."

"What were you responding to then?" he said amiably.

"Oh sweetie I told you—I just liked you, was all. But you *are* terribly correct, Lewis. And then, the way you are, I didn't see how you could possibly not have a girl in New York. And then anyway you were going to be here only this day or two, weren't you? *Have* you a New York girl?"

"Good god," he complained, "what a question to sound honest replying to!"

"But do you have?"

Dammit he said *no!* California either!

"... When was the last one."

"But look," he said mildly, "what was all that about I-wasn't-to-be-stupid-and-jealous, a couple of nights ago?"

"I'm not being! Can't I be tenderly anxious about you?"

"That what your generation calls it?"

"Oh sweet don't hedge! When was she?"

Oh, well, he said, last winter.

"Winter ending in March?"

... Easter'd been late, this year.

"You mean it isn't really over at all?" she cried.

Oh yes. She'd got a job in Washington. Look, this was the daughter of a client. Three or four years ago—

"It began *four years ago?*"

No no no *no*, the girl was still in college then, simply he'd let her what's called 'intern' during summer vacation, to oblige her father. She was an economics major. Been no question of! Affairs in the office?—at *his* age?

"So then *what?*"

. . . Oh well, the usual thing, call it, what else? An affair. After that summer he hadn't seen her, till one day last autumn she'd rung him up. Might she interview him professionally? Because she was doing a piece, for some learned journal or other, on 'the metapolitics of stock-options.' Or some such, and if she took him to lunch could she pick his brains about it a little?

"You hadn't seen her in all that time?"

Or thought of. No occasion to. Been several years. Four, even. But anyway. You did get this sort of request, how not. Clients could ask you to do a talk on the market, for instance, at their club. He'd even done a couple of guest lectures at Yale. So he had lunch with the girl.

"And went on from there!" she accused him.

No no no no, at lunch all they—

"She didn't have somebody already?—in her *twenties?*—in New *York?*"

What if she had? Hardly the sort of question he—

"What was she like?"

. . . What was anybody!

"That's not what I meant!"

But dammit she'd asked him, hadn't she?—and in so many words!—whether he ever 'took off after' people. He was only describ—

"So you did go after her!"

. . . In a light-hearted way, yes, why not?

"You didn't after *me!*"

"What *is* all this?" he cried. "How's a simple man to conduct himself if not on the, what's one to call it? the hypotheses of egotism and experience? There are too many ways the average young man can exasperate a young woman for her not to be looking for a lover she hopes won't. If the fellow's catnip of course there's nothing immediate to be done—she has to be silly and get it over with. She has to discover that all catnip is is catnip. But aside from that—"

"So you mean you just heartlessly dispossessed some helpless young man she had!"

"'Heartlessly'!"

"He could have been some terribly easily hurt mere *boy!*"

"But dammit my angel it was *she* that—"

"Didn't you ever even meet him, to find out?"

"What would I do a cockeyed thing like meet him for!—compare our perquisites and prerogatives?"

"But Lewis you don't just—"

He had, once, *heard* the guy. Sort of, anyway. This'd been late one night; poor guy'd rung her bell. She was up on her arm in an instant, furiously listening. Then he'd rung again, and she'd breathed *Oh damn* and sprung out of bed and off into the little hall, and he'd heard the faint rattle of the door-chain, and then the mumble of their voices, on and on. . . . Though God bless, what can either side say that makes sense in *that* situation! Finally of course she sent him away. But he'd heard the rise and fall of their voices a long while first. Then she came softly back to him in the dark. As if nothing much had happened, come to think of it. So that was that.

". . . Not even a *little* upset?"

"*I* was upset. Look, I felt badly for him! If you lose a girl you lose her, but dear god you might as well go hang yourself as mope and maunder around keeping tabs on whatever unappetizing lout she's replaced you with! Maybe he'd been waiting across somewhere in the shadows, hour after hour, to see whether oh please God *not!* —the impossible off-chance that when she came home at last she'd come home alone. Except there she had come home with me. And I'd gone in with her. And he'd seen the light in her apartment go on. And then (and soon) go out. And there he might have been standing on and on, in the black night of the soul, seeing in his mind how perhaps at that very instant every lovely inch of her— There's an anguished couplet of Ovid's, my angel, that says it all: 'multa miser timeo—I shake at what he may do with you for I have done it all myself—my own damned example has me on the rack!' How can a man *let* himself be caught like that? And what low Plautine streak in human nature ever decided the locked-out lover was a stock figure for farce? 'Mens abit, et morior'—and you *might* as well be dead! That night, I was appalled. . . ."

"But you went heartlessly right back to making love with her didn't you?" she rebuked him.

"As a matter of fact," he said, "no, I didn't."

"Oh Lewis *truly* didn't?"

"Dammit I was upset!"

So she gazed at him as if decoding this. And finally said, "But I didn't think men felt like that."

Maybe in her generation they didn't.

"No I mean the way you felt. About him."

Why shouldn't he have? Roman comedy or not!

"But how did she feel?"

He said, amused, 'd hardly felt he knew the young lady well enough to ask.

"No be *serious*," she begged him. "Because after my husband— Well, I'd left him, I'd moved to the pied-à-terre my mother has on the East River, sweetie I told you, there was this man I fell in love with, was why. Because the way I'd found I felt about him, oh Lewis if I'd stayed, my husband's just *being* there would remind me of the, the, of the difference, and change all the other feelings perhaps I'd had about him *ever!* And when I'd felt I thought so fond of him so long, having to face don't you see whether really *had* I! And perhaps only feel sad about him. Because getting used to myself with somebody new—Oh dear why am I *discussing* this with you!"

He said agreeably ah then don't. And in any case, you put everything you'd discovered about love (including a random infidelity only the night before) into each new affair, so why shouldn't each be better than the last?

"Am *I?* Or goodness, am I! Because put *that* way, what does it mean I am?" she protested, and began to laugh at him. "Oh Lewis what a way to look at things! Because then isn't some horrid girl going to replace me for your benefit as easily as I seem to have replaced your last little— *Had* she been with him the night before?"

No no, all he'd meant was—

"Well but are you saying you expect to go effortlessly on and on with these convenient replacements?—and, each time, each of us in this endless series is a, is a what? an improvement? on the one before?"

So naturally he snorted. Was she out of her perverse head? The 'improvement' he'd meant was, obviously, they improved *him*, what on earth else! It was women men learned manners from wasn't it? And always had been. Bedroom and drawing-room both. So why *not* the more the better? And if the way he was (at the peak of his perfection) appealed to her, he said laughing, then what was there for her to fuss at?

"But sweet so uninterruptedly *many!*"

He said but—

"I hate them *all*," she said contentedly; and as this was hardly

what they were talking about in any case, they left the theory of the
thing, for the rest of that evening at least, unannotated further.

∞

But next day, sure enough, Sather came back to his hotel to
change for lunch, and there were these messages the concierge
handed him with his key.

The day before, a Mr. Bingham had telephoned Monsieur; the
message left was that Mr. Newman had returned to Paris.

The day before, a Mr. Newman had telephoned Monsieur; the
message left was that he had returned to Paris and would telephone
Monsieur in the morning.

This morning a Mr. Newman had telephoned Monsieur; he had
left a number, which would Monsieur have the kindness, at Monsieur's convenience, to call.

This number however, when he rang it, did not answer.

When moreover he then rang Bingham's extension at the Embassy, a voice like a caress breathed Oh was this Mr. Sather? for
then Mr. Bingham was not in but had left a message for Monsieur in
case Monsieur called, and this was that Mr. Newman was back in
Paris, and would call him.

So when Maria picked him up for lunch she said, "Oh damn,
now you'll be going home!"

And when she hadn't had even a quarter enough of him!

He said well but God bless, 'home'?—she forget the job he was
here for? These polite embassies took time. You didn't disentangle a
young man from the pretty arms round his neck just overnight.
Could take a week. *Could* take a fortnight.

But suppose it didn't.

And even if it did, what was going to happen then? They both
knew what was going to happen then!

He said but—

And when here they were with a love in their laps!

But dear god—

It was *sad* to think that his dismal 'making do' was all he had to look forward to!

With she supposed the next wandering wife or teenage economist he happened on? . . .

But at lunch in the Rue du Bac (this restaurant had she said been gutted and *completely* refitted and tarted up a couple of years ago, but was now would he believe it as classically what the French called 'loyal' as if it still had its dotty old painted tin ceiling)—at lunch she said simply what he should *do* was open why not a branch in Paris. His clients needed foreign titres too in their portfolios didn't they? and he'd get new clients here, and expand. And hadn't he seen, as to amenities, how much simply better one lived here? He'd have the lovely life he ought to have—France was *France!* "And then of course also," she ended it, and laughed, "I could have you and *have* you!"

He said a Paris office? God bless!—when he hadn't a word of French?

"When you've *me?*" she cried—not to mention all the other fundamental amenities. Which she lovingly listed: nobody bothered you; there were proper domestics still; the bread, once you had found *the* boulangerie in your quarter, was a supreme food; the tax situation had been made advantageous beyond Republican dreams; the wine hadn't had to travel; the trains ran.

And *no* one (she said in tender mockery) would be lurking in the shadows of her street to see how she came home.

So there. And he could réfléchir. . . .

But when she dropped him at his hotel to change for dinner, there was the message. A Mr. Newman had telephoned: could Monsieur be informed that Mr. Newman was driving a friend down into Normandy tomorrow for lunch, and would Monsieur be free to join them. Mr. Newman would be by about ten in the morning. He urgently hoped he would find Monsieur free.

So it now confronted them.

—Though at dinner, and this, again, they had on that terrasse of his hotel, the summer dusk already deepening into night over the fading gardens off into the black leaves of the lindens beyond, so that the massed flaming of a hundred candles, table by damask'd table, made it as if a low pavilion of light without walls had been built out under those vaults of darkness; or again it could have been a lighted proscenium stood out there, set for the staging of a play, and the actors there, and in that soft brilliance, above the crystal and silver of the tables, the eyes of actresses would be like jewels as they looked at you—at dinner then Maria was gently exploring consequences.

"Darling tell me something?"

So he looked need-she-ask.

"About if you come back. *Do* I mean decide. To open this office."

He said hypotheses, huh.

"Tell me anyway?"

He snorted mildly.

"Because I don't want to upset you," she said lightly, "but it's about how I feel."

'Upset' him!

"Yes but it *may!*" she cried. "Anyway *something!* Because I told you—I don't think I know how to deal with this, not any way at all. I'm beginning to be afraid I've got you rather badly. Of course *that* I don't think you'd mind, but I've— Oh Lewis I'm *not* possessive, but I keep thinking about your past with love and terror, how can I help it, so if you do come back will you mind if now and then I'm jealous of your ghosts?"

He said, sounding amused, but what earthly sort of hypothetical anxiety—

"But aren't you even a little jealous of mine?"

Hardly told him God bless enough, had she, to be jealous about! Including about for instance this chap she'd said she'd left her husband for.

"Oh but sweetie simply I lost my head about him, what else, what d'you think, what *does* one do, heavens!" she passed this off with. "Didn't *you* ever feel you suddenly wanted somebody more than you'd ever wanted anything on earth?"

Catnip, huh!

"Don't laugh—it's lovely!" she said; and that was that.

—Later, though, in the contented midnight of their bed ("Mind if you don't seduce me again for a little?" "Only keep us awake anyhow"), half entangled still, lips idly grazing his shoulder, ". . . or anyway lost my head *enough*," she murmured, conceding. "Because I guess I half didn't know what was happening to me. You know? The first time I made love with him, and I never had, then, with anybody but my husband, well, the difference of course, but it was the, oh the *discovery*, Lewis! I'd *never* imagined anyone could make you feel like that, and then to have to leave the heaven of those few vanishing hours, so rushing and gone, and go back to— And oh I blew it, I made a scene about *nothing*—and I'd felt so lovely, coming from him, that I thought how easy to feel tender about my husband too, and then I came in and there he was, and I thought but I never *saw* how he was till now—and oh poor darling I blew up, oh Lewis so *sad!*"

. . . Past consoling, he said. And always had been.

"But you," she said, "you're the same thing, only worse, it's like being stunned. Because one never believes how it turns out it is. And stunned twice over, because the bliss of it, that *anything* can be so overwhelming, and then thinking but what is it, how *can* it be what it is! So you're dazed all over again," she mumbled, through a rosy mouthful of his neck. "Do men ever feel like this too?"

Why, for him at least, yes, he said. Or anyhow, when this happened, somehow one was in it, part of the girl's tumult. Not that it always happened—as things stood between the sexes still, women seemed to be wary of giving in to their senses. For that did, he'd concede, change the whole history of the self for them. Which could upset anybody. So they didn't get what was called 'involved.' For instance, had she with this Bingham?

She whirled up onto her elbow and stared at him, speechless.

Well, he said, had she?

". . . How did you know!" she cried at him.

Guessed. How else.

"But Lewis *how?*"

All the denying.

So she drooped, saying, ". . . oh." And as she then collapsed humbly onto him again, for some time they lay there in silence.

Till presently she said, *"Does* it upset you?"

. . . Oh, well, he supposed a little. In his generation you rather—

"But sweet I wasn't in *love* with Jock! I was just getting over the, the taste of the other affair. And Jock was attractive and amusing. And *nice.* And it wasn't an affair—it was *nothing* like this with you, nobody's been. Goodness, I only made love with him two or three times, you *can't* be jealous about that!"

He said look, dammit, it was man's simple-mindedness made these things a complexity. To see a girl's body in memory was one thing, and you could endure it, but the dazzling reality of it, tangible and *there,* and past belief temporarily yours, reduced you to idiocy.

So why shouldn't the revolting idea that some low lecher of a peasant—

"He wasn't! He was sweet!"

Catnip, huh.

". . . No."

So (he snickered) she'd passed him on to her partner?

". . . Sweetie that *isn't* the nicest way to put it!"

The terminology matter? Ah, well, they were a hair-raising sex. His old uncle used to say, 'Women are women—and it's just as well.' Whatever that meant.

But she said, "And anyway you haven't any right to say anything about it. All those *Sather* girls! They're all alike—and then they come back for more! And that's all you think about us! I should never make love with you again!" she mumbled, kissing him.

But dear god who'd been patiently hearing about her men?— and in quantity!

"But Lewis I was *explaining* myself to you, is all, what d'you think! And I haven't had anything like your disgusting dozens, so there!"

So, in perhaps amusement, they were silent.

Till presently she murmured, ". . . J'ai la gorge comme on les demande?"

. . . What'd that mean.

"Oh what a stupid amant, what have I done to deserve so uninstructed a man in bed with me!" she cried at him. "Un amant qui n'a même pas de bribes de français! Where your *hand* is, my darling! Or are you jealous of my ghosts?"

. . . Ghosts were for an age when they still upset you. Natural enough!—you wanted to be able to think it was only You the lovely thing had ever been like this with, or wanted to be. But at any age it was a kind of sadness.

"... Even not needing to? When was *never* this but you?"

So he muttered something gentlemanly. To which however she paid no attention; for now, as if from some musing midnight of her own, she had begun to tell him, it seemed, how it began.

"Because oh sweet," she said, lips against his throat, "it was the way I found I was thinking about you, and so soon. Thought about you I mean when I was undressing. At night. Or should I tell you, and spoil you more. Because I'd think what it would be like, if you were there, watching. What it would do to you. And what having you watching would do to me. And when oh dear I'd only known you two days! Oh but how wishing you were there, because then— Oh well how was I to know we were going to seduce each other so adorably? Oh anyway, *here!*" she ordered, and rolling up from his shoulder she gave him a long kiss. "There—that's to keep my rope on you! And tomorrow in Normandy you'll *buy off* this 'friend' of your Mr. Newman's—promise?" she ended contentedly, "not just charm her?"

He said *god* no.

—It was deep dawn, that morning, when he left, her little street already silver with it, and the Avenue, full day. At her gate he turned to smile goodby. She was standing in the half-open doorway, head leaning against the jamb, looking at him almost somberly; but as he smiled, with a sudden fierce gravity she said, *"I love you!"*— and was gone.

Because, said like that, it is a spell.

3

Ah! par pitié, Madame, daignez calmer le trouble de mon âme;
daignez m'apprendre ce que je dois espérer ou craindre.

—LACLOS, *Les Liaisons Dangereuses*

. . . avec un coeur de la trempe du sien, un coeur noble et vertueux,
une jeune femme comme celle-là, quand on lui parle d'amour, n'a
point d'autre parti à prendre que de fuir. Si elle s'amuse à se scan-
daliser tout bas du compliment qu'on lui fait, l'air soumis d'un
amant la gagne, son ton pénétré la blesse, et je la garantis perdue
quinze jours après.

—MARIVAUX, *Le Spectateur Français*

Elle ne pouvoit s'empêcher d'être troublée de sa vue . . . mais, quand
elle ne le voyoit plus . . . elle n'eut pas néanmoins la force: il y avoit
trop longtemps qu'elle ne l'avoit vu, pour se résoudre à ne le voir pas.

—MME. DE LA FAYETTE, *La Princesse de Clèves*

I never thought he would ring up that second time, and ask
again.

And *never*, how I would feel.

So how possibly should I have been sur mes gardes. Folly, yes:
c'est normal. But against that *instantaneous* wild mingling of exalta-
tion and dismay? . . .

Or to have set the phone back on its stand again faint with
happiness notwithstanding?

Baudouin came out of his dressing-room saying, "Ton américain?" and I heard my voice say, "Mais oui," without the slightest

quaver; and he came across behind me at the dressing-table and I leaned my head back against him and closed my eyes and said, "Ah mon Dieu, Chad and I should never have fed the polite man lunch!" And he said, "Jeu de revanche, que veux-tu," and bent and kissed the nape of my neck where I love, and down along into the hollow of my shoulder, and I brushed my cheek against his and said, "So I do mon cher have to let him feed me," thinking *though what shall I find it is I have beyond help said yes to.* "Mais tu sors?" I said, and he said, "Que dans le quartier," and I said, "Tu rentres quand?" and he said, "Mais te chercher!" and kissed the top of my head with love and smiled at me in the dressing-glass, and was gone.

I picked up my brush and began to brush my hair again, and I could not even think what I was doing.

—But what was I to have said.

With not even an instant to think! And with Baudouin là à côté, no farther than his dressing-room.

—Ah, but still!—*why* that half-fainting yes. . . .

And when he had not even been plausible, 'mon américain'! What sort of reason for asking me again was 'before he left France'? And yet I accepted it! As if it had been a reasoned whim of my own! I *accepted* it!

Because ah what could he I suppose have said that would have been 'reasonable' enough—it was reason that would have given me reason to refuse. . . .

—Ah, and anyway!

It was his voice. Asking.

—Alors bon, there *was* no reason I could have accepted and I knew it, voilà, the first syllable he spoke I knew it, I was *done* with reason, it was his voice. I looked at my brushing image in the glass and said to her, aloud, "Et si tu n'es plus à défendre? . . ."

And how can he not know. He has been loved too often not to

know. That day at the domaine, even, he knew. And, now, it is five days of knowledge more.

". . . enchantment," he said that day, at the end, the sun on his hair as he bowed over my cold fingers, the sunflooded stone of the manoir towering over us, the dreaming summer of the gardens around us and beyond, but it was I l'ensorcelée, the spellbound. And even then, beyond saving, fascinée . . .

Though how should he know? Or a mere polite Yes tell him! And when couldn't the man simply feel he owes me a luncheon?—alors qu'il s'en acquitte! Is a polite accession to his American sense of what shall I call it? of social obligations a capitulation dans les formes? Am I in a panic for *that*?

And think how he himself must have felt, coming to 'rescue' Chad but finding *me!* For oh the poor man, the absolute awfulness of his embassy, the sheer malappris of it, and now he knows it. He was I admit impeccable; even that first moment in the hotel court-yard in Versailles, not the flicker of an eyelid. And of course he will not bring it up, across a table from me at the Plaza-Athénée or any-where else. But it will *be* there, in his mind—an uneasiness, a chagrin, un malencontreux, a wordless hope of appeasing.

—Ah but he *knows*. He knew that day at the domaine. And again in my mind I saw the homage in his eyes as we said goodby, and that glint too of—was it almost appraisal? as he turned with Chad and they went into the manoir and through it to Chad's car in the courtyard and away. I was lost, and he knew. I looked into my terrified eyes in the glass and that too I said aloud, "Il le *sait*. . . ."

But what if he does know—is *he* a man who would let me see he does, or amuse himself with the knowledge? Ah he could not be so cynical!—il est *bien*, he has been loved often because he has de-served to be loved, or he could not be what he is. Enfin qu'il sache!

—am I to be other than myself whether or not he knows? I shall be
as safe in the court of the Plaza-Athénée as—

The phone rang.

I think I had been going to add the proviso *à moins de folie*, but
oh it was so sudden and imperious, the phone, just when every nerve-
end in my body was vibrating with the imminence of him, that who
could I think it was if not he?—though why *again?* why possibly?
was luncheon off and I was *not* to see him? It rang again, and then
again, and even when I did at last pick it up and said allô, all I was
thinking was what could I think of to say.

But when it was *Jock*, I was so dizzy with deliverance that I said,
"Oh Jock it was *you?*" like a child.

"What's this was-me?" he said cheerfully. "*Is*-me is how I'd
hoped my friends thought about me, what's the matter with you!
And as it happens I'm at the *very* top of my form. I am breathing
down the neck of my time. In fact I've just helped the ambassador
cut a couple career throats he's had his eye on for most of the year.
'Why call on God in His great mercy to strike the bastards down,' I
said to him, 'when you can do it yourself with a budget?' God's
mercies aren't thunderbolts anyway, I told him, just something to be
thankful for at intervals. Rather a second-rate sort of thing to base
One's reputation on, between you and me—especially if One has tri-
personally caused what the mercy's needed for. Yes. Well. Not what
I rang up about. I gather Chad's perhaps told you our Mr. Sather
has what's called been by, and that Chad is wanted home, d'urgence,
for purposes of family empire."

So I must have said yes how sad, for he said, " 'Sad'?—but from
Chad I gathered you practically said how wonderful for him! Are
you heartless? Heartless you are, and what's more, poor chap, you
aren't even letting him come round and argue."

"Ah but you *know*," I said, "how Baudouin is, on leaves. And I am devoted to him. And I did you know tell you. At lunch. At Barbizon. I *told* you."

"Ah, well," he said, "let me at least put you in the current picture? Because look, Fabienne my angel, I am doing my disabused best for you *and* for him. I am not Corneille, knocking out couplets on love and duty like so many fungoes, but I *have* been doing the facts of life in short beginner's takes. If some angel tells you she adores you (I say to him) why not believe her? Saves argument. Anyhow girls fall in love with us from time to time don't they?— with an air of selectivity, too! So why *not* conclude they know what they're doing? But in the contrary case therefore *also* (I remind him) the principle obtains: if she is done she is done. As my in-house composer put it, a couple of her ballades ago—

I do not love thee, sweetie-pie.
The reason *why*'s the reason why.

God help me, I've even cited the classics for his enlightenment— remember Aphrodite I said in the Homeric hymn? There she was, in the first faint shadows of dawn, eeling stealthily out of bed and tiptoe-ing into her clothes—never wanted to see the fellow again, what *had* she been doing in bed with a mortal!—and what does this back-country peasant of an Anchises do but wake up and gawk at her! What girl wouldn't fling into a fury, goddess or not! 'Aásthen!' she spits at him. 'To think *I* was infatuated! The whole *thing* skhétlion ouk onomaston—so awful there isn't a word for it! I was out of my *mind*!' And if the oaf ever so much as mentioned— Ah, well, aásthen. Very funny, 'infatuated,' from a goddess whose specialty was infatuation! But not the kind of language you like to hear about a friend."

—But I was hardly I think listening.

Because I can never, really, can I (I was saying to myself) explain what has happened to me. Is happening. How could anyone explain. There is no language to. It is from some ancient chaos before language. Even if I could find words that would explain it exactly as it feels it *is*, it would not be explained.

But Jock was saying, ". . . so I have been *torn* over it! I am on the side of all of you. Comme un benêt. Inconduite and all. But you I adore, and I have put up with my irrelevant reservations. The finality of divine planning is final, I say to myself, but think—*we* are the demonstration? So shall I ring you? I'll ring you."

He hung up, and I picked up my brush again.

—If it stays cool, I thought, I will wear that two-piece summer silk I got chez Goulnár; and I saw it in my mind, the ribbing at the wrists and throat, and where the sleeves are set into the sleek shoulders it is like épaulières in court armor, really *very* elegant, and anyway in that kind of blouson I look inabordable. Baudouin even said on te croirait dans les affaires, and I haven't worn it since.

Tant pis. It is elegant.

And why should I not be.

I will walk there, I thought, brushing. The Avenue Montaigne is barely ten minutes. And in a taxi I should dither. Walking, my heart will beat as if I were only walking, I said to my image in the glass, softly brushing; and after a little, Baudouin came in again, to fetch me, and we went to his mother's, off the Place d'Iéna. My heart beating as if I were only walking.

But in the morning it had turned hot.

So if he should have reserved a courtyard table at the Plaza-Athénée, what to wear.

I tried to remember the court. But when had I had luncheon there, anyway in summer? Or had I ever. Ah mon Dieu I couldn't remember that either! It could be anything. Including *not* a table in the court! Then how was I to know what to dress for! Why of *all* places had he had to settle on a banality like the Plaza-Athénée! How was I expected to decide *what* to wear!

Ah zut I'd wear just something sleeveless then, who cared! And if 'accessible,' tant pis!

And walk anyway. Me détendre. A *slow* ten minutes. Timed to be late un petit quart d'heure.

(Though heavens the way Baudouin had wheedled and courted me *this* leave, how could I not be détendue! . . .)

Désinvolte, anyway, when the time came—so full of the noontide brilliance of the Quai de Passy that I was nearly at the Port Debilly before I thought am I too soon?—and I was, there was the Pont de l'Alma, ah zut I was going to be almost à l'heure. Or only five minutes late at the most. And one can't *saunter*—should I decently kill time and go up the Avenue Georges V first? and across to the Avenue Montaigne at the level of the, of what *is* that first little— Or should I take the street next beyond and come out in the Avenue Montaigne above the hotel instead? Or what?

Oh or *what*?

But then abruptly oh thank God (I could have crossed myself in deliverance right there on the quai!) I thought but am I une petite nigaude de seize ans, in Heaven's name, and this my first rendezvous I am headed for, quailing? I was in such a pet at myself I began walking faster still, à grands pas even—very well I'd *be* on time then! Let him think what he liked!—tôt venu tôt en fait even, if he liked, and wonder why! And I would cut the luncheon short too if I thought *he*—if I pleased. At the Place de l'Alma I didn't so much as glance up the Avenue Georges V as I passed it.

But then, turning into the Avenue Montaigne, I did, a little, slow down. In three minutes, in two, I should find him waiting in any case. And discover how he looked. This time I would make sure. I can hardly have glanced at him, at Versailles. I was expecting un fâcheux quelconque, how not. Helping Chad get rid of him, en faisant l'aimable; how he looked mattered no more than he. And it was deep shade under the lindens. I didn't really *see* him at all. Until after we started, and I turned round ...

—Anyway now what was left me but a scène à faire he must know by heart! Which *I* had now to play as innocently as if I could never guess how innocently how many women had played it for him a hundred times before. ...

Then there at the hotel he was, coming tall and courtly to meet me the instant I stepped into the doorway, coming straight at me saying my name as if it were a delight to, a deliverance to—but I was so overcome by my awareness of him, so daunted, that I must have stopped halfway in, mindless, for what was I even to say to this man I knew I should need every defense against, why had I not *thought* what I could say?—only had I even the breath to? but then there he was, before me, saying but *how* kind it was of me to have relented and met him like this but had I *walked* here? said so naturally that without having to think I found myself answering bonjour but heavens how *not* walk, in the lovely noon! and in any case we lived practically à côté, in Passy; and I was breathing again. And he could have noticed nothing, it was so swift and over. And as we went on in toward the courtyard I could even add (and almost lightly, now!), "And I am even on time for you, Mr. Sather! —or do American women go to the trouble of spoiling you too. ..."

But how easy! An omen.

And at the table I found I could even look at him. Also there was champagne ready in a cooler, and he had the sommelier at once there opening it.

Then, it was amusing, translating things on the menu for him—for how could anyone be dangerous, so helpless! And over the rim of the glass I could look at him and be free.

Except how could I any longer, I said to myself, sipping, quite see him even as I had at the last there, up the sun-dappled lawns at the domaine, hardly knowing what I did, in the wild tumult of my dismay, except I knew I must never see him again. And ah, *then*, still thinking I could bear it! Though what mon Dieu was I doing now but tell myself I was bearing it—watching the play of light and expression on his face as he ordered and the captain bent over him, the poise of his head, the glints of grey at his temples, the look of his mouth, the way his tanned fingers held the carte; and I drank off my glass and thought in two short hours at the most I shall rise smiling from this table and thank him for his repas and his amabil-ités and wish him a smiling bon voyage home, and turn on my stylish heels la mort dans l'âme, and *not* ever see him again.

Et j'en prends déjà le deuil, I said deep in my mind, and if when you telephoned I did not ask why you wished to see me once more, it was because I did not dare to: what could you have said but 'to repay my kindness'? and what was that for me to have *had* to say yes to! and he finished ordering and I fluttered a finger at my glass for the man to fill.

So delicious, I said; and had Chad I hoped been seeing to him properly?

And he said oh very competently. Much improved, he'd found. Hardly barbarian now at all.

So he'd been able to dispense with his—what did she call herself? his 'courier'?

Well, not altogether, he said, no. He couldn't after all expect Chad to drop everything and turn cicerone. So Mrs. Godfrey was still very kindly shepherding him about. A very knowledgeable young woman.

"But didn't you feel a little odd, Mr. Sather," I said, " 'hiring' a pretty girl to go about with you day and night? Or isn't she pretty enough to matter."

Oh, being 'pretty,' he said easily, was just part of the job anywhere, wasn't it? And then, a thing like beauty, anyway!—it always lay in wait there, in women. Like a beckoning ghost. Of course if you saw her somehow and followed, you were lost. No, but what he'd been in plain fact enchanted by was France itself, the way it seemed we lived here, the whole ambience. The intelligence; the freedom. It had been a—well, simply it had come over him *this* was how he wished he were living himself. Matter of fact, he said, he'd wondered why shouldn't he? At least a part of the time. He had a branch office he visited in San Francisco; why not one in Paris?

But oh dear Heaven he must *not!*—and I said, "But Mr. Sather you don't even understand French!"

He said what of it?—be for his American clients, not French. He'd been thinking for months anyhow they ought to be getting into European investment more. Europe's sheer exasperation with these endless and *total* American foreign-policy ineptitudes, for instance, was going to *end* in the Common Market's taking off on its own, how not? And that meant far more money to be made for his clients in European companies than at home. Not to mention tax advantages! So a Paris office was easy to justify economically. And as to 'spiritually,' he said, smiling, he'd found France didn't need justifying. So he had been making a few inquiries. If only to see.

Then he said it: "If I should come, Madame, might I hope to be allowed to pay my respects to you, and, well, now and then perhaps see you again?"—and suddenly he was looking straight into my eyes.

As when I'd turned round that morning in the car . . .

And this time too I suppose I could say I looked a moment too long. Ah, but this time?—*this* time I knew what had happened to me, and dear Heaven was he as near to being sure it had as this?—for him to come back to?—and he was *asking?*

But he was saying, almost humbly, "I realize I could hardly God help me have had a more unfortunate introduction to you. I came on an errand I ought never to have undertaken to start with. I never would have, if I'd known it concerned someone like you. But even without knowing, I should never have."

I must *stop him!* I said, "But my dear Mr. Sather you haven't been désobligeant in the least!"

But wasn't he even listening to me? For oh, he went *on* with it!—couldn't he *see* I mustn't care *what* he explained his feelings were? He'd begun (he said) to realize how out of place Americans can be, abroad; what outsiders. Perhaps always had been—he'd been haunted, in Versailles, by a sad adventure of Thomas Jefferson's there, at the court of Louis XVI. This had been before our Revolution—Jefferson'd been America's ambassador. A fashionable English painter was in Versailles at the time, doing miniatures of court beauties, a man named Cosway; he was about Jefferson's age, and he had the usual delicious painter's wife, a talented musician and painter herself—"but also, Madame, Maria Cosway was only in her mid-twenties, and our Mr. Jefferson was alas on his way toward fifty, so you can imagine the man's helpless desperation when he found himself in love with her—Jefferson, who was eighteenth-century Reason in person!"

I watched the blue of his eyes change as his head moved, and I thought Can I believe I am hearing this, the taste of tears in my throat?—ces frivolités d'archiviste, the one time I shall ever have been alone with him?

But he was saying, ". . . letter he wrote to her afterwards, of how he saw her off for England, from the Pavillon de St. Denis. 'I handed you into your carriage,' he says, 'and watched the wheels begin to revolve and slowly bear you away from me. And I turned on my heel, more dead than alive, and walked across the Pavillon to my carriage. And had myself driven back into Paris I cared not where.' It's I suppose a rather plain eighteenth-century style. Byron a quarter century later would have said 'death in my heart' instead. And I know I have no right, Madame, to afflict you with any of this anyway. Even if you have perhaps had the generosity to sense my feelings but forgive them. But when I think of not seeing you ever again, as poor Jefferson never again saw Maria Cosway, I find I am more dead than alive too."

—For an instant I thought I should faint: the court was a spinning dazzle. Ah Dieu du Ciel I was saved, I was *safe*, he was as stricken as I, I could do as I pleased with him, there were not even bienséances, I was *free!* . . . The dizziness vanished, and I could see his face again, and my eyes said I hardly know what except 'I am *not* yours, oh lovely lovely . . .' and that awful trembling was gone as if it had never been; and I thought 'Encore est vive la souris!'

And oh what a surcroît de bonheur, to have given me this too!—to sweetly torment him with, to tenderly pity him for, to live remembering he had said, to be sometimes dazed, remembering . . .

Oh and no longer to care or have to care what I said or what I did or what he thought! Or what *I* thought—for there were no more bienséances, or if there were it should be *I* who had created them, ah I almost laughed aloud in the pure happiness of my deliverance. . . .

For oh what a lovely game now too! and I said, "But Mr. Sather what am I to say!" (And what could he, poor man!) "Because *this*,

Monsieur?—if you understood French I would tell you qu'il revient de l'autre côté de l'inouï!"

Oh but the poor man how stuffy I sounded. And besides not understanding what I said he looked too miserable to answer anyway, so I was cruel too! so as if just amused I said, "But surely this can't be how Americans go about seducing a virtuous wife? On nous fait la cour, oui—even fall in love with us now and then I'm told, to make it more convincing. But *this* quantum leap, Mr. Sather?—to expect me to think you in despair over me after a country luncheon and a quarter-hour of our mere second meeting?"

So at least he tried to smile. "But God help me," he said, "would I put myself in this insufferable position, or subject you of all people, Madame, to the dejecting spectacle of it, if I weren't near the end of desperation? I haven't even Jefferson's eighteenth-century belief in Order, to sustain me. I *am* in despair. I am not even plausible to myself. For all I know the Count is the most charming husband in France."

Of course *some* bienséances must be preserved—one automatically says, "I forbid you to speak of him!" (And anyway!—*that* sort of remark! And so soon!)

But naturally he said, "But for that matter what can there be, Madame, that you can't irreproachably forbid me? I am appalled at myself myself! How am I *not* to appear to you a man his enchantment with you has reduced to the effrontery of hope?"

Oh, he delighted me! " 'Effrontery'?" I said. "On devient donc hardi par ses espérances?—you are even beginning to sound eighteenth-century yourself!" I said laughing. "Even dans les règles, Mr. Sather! You look so ready to sigh that it could serve you in place of sighing. But do think what you are asking me to believe!"

"But what else do you think I have been in despair over, Madame," he cried, "if not the hopelessness of asking you to believe me! My difficulty is the *difficulty!* Can a man ever really think up anything less simple-minded to say to a woman he adores than why *not* fall in love with him, what good does it do not to? God bless, what fatuity!"

"But what would happen to us, Mr. Sather," I said, "if you were all as charming as the way you look makes us think you are? A man doesn't know what he does. And that is désobligeant. And *that* is really what saves us—it's no trouble at all keeping one's head if one's not being tempted to lose it very expertly indeed! No but what are you doing really, Mr. Sather," I said. "When you came, you had the, what shall I call it? the malhonnêteté to assume it seems it was *I*, not France, that was keeping Chad from his factories—imagine! And now you're proposing to make the same insulting mistake yourself in reverse? and come to France for *me?*—what *are* you doing!"

He said, " 'Doing'? In my indefensible predicament what is there a man can do! Ovid wrote a brilliant treatise once on how to re-cover, and simply from regard for your feelings God knows I should like to, but what if text-book remedies don't apply? 'Sceleratae facta puellae' is the basic maxim: remember 'the things the damn' girl's done to you.' But you're not some wretched girl, you're an angel—and what you've done to me, Madame, whether you choose to know it or not, is dazzle me, daze me, enchant me, en—"

"You must not *say* such things to me!" I said. "Hardi or not, you must not! You *know* you must not! You are making it impossible for me!"—but I heard the caress in my voice as I said it, and I thought aïe I've said it *wrong*, am I so light-headed with relief still that I have let myself *forget* what has happened to me? And the danger? "Are you pretending not to be a text-book case, Mr. Sather," I said, "be-cause a text-book remedy doesn't cure you?—heavens, what a con-venient logic!"

But what was I to do with the poor man?—he still it seemed couldn't smile; he was tragic, oh he was lovely! He said, "But that morning in Versailles I wasn't expecting *you*, Madame! Or what happened to me. Or the way it happened—the thunderclap! In my *life* I'd never— Your beauty was like a dagger glittering to its mark. Are you really so heartless as not to care what you do? Or even to bother to notice? There in the courtyard of the hotel you hardly so much as glanced at me!"

"Do you expect women to gaze in your eyes and be lost, Mr. Sather?" I said, laughing at him. "Why on earth should I have more than glanced, with all the day ahead to look at you and be stricken!"

"But all the way down to Normandy," he said—

"But I was down out of the wind, what else!—you *saw* how Chad drives!" I said. "Surely you weren't staring at me?—but then how mannerless and flattering! But ah Mr. Sather do let's be sensible. You adore me so convincingly you must be a libertine born—in another five minutes you will be able to charm me into anything you please, I shall be lost. But must I really feel you are lost too? Do let me cajole you into being honest!"

So at least he began to smile. 'Honest'? he said—was anything as deranged as infatuation to have moral responsibilities supposed of it? For the matter of that, was he to think it was honesty women were susceptible to, instead of flattery?

"You say that and flatter anyway?" I said.

But if men didn't flatter us, we'd be certain they were in love with somebody else, wouldn't we?—so why not, he said—and now he was almost laughing.

—Oh mon américain que vous me plaisez. . . .

Except . . . am I really to forget that a man as assured and urbane as this man is, ah mon Dieu and as plausible!—For *imagine* 'speaking out' after no more than a mere—And as if so overcome he was helpless not to! Oh I am faint with admiration at him, at simply how he made it sound, how *reasonable* he makes me feel I should be, believing him! oh I could fall in love with the danger of him all over again, with the tour de force of it, of what it does to me!

And then, anyway, really *is* it so . . . unheard of? For are you (I thought) 'desperate' perhaps truly, mon bel américain? and *that* is why? . . .

I will never ask. To ask says everything. And poses questions who could let herself believe the mockery of answers to, and of his answers above all.

For has a man like this man no New York girl to leave behind— and unexplained to!—if (again and again) he should come to an office here? leave behind moping or sulking or fuming, or simply in tears? Leave and come to *me* from? And go back to?

Or even have here perhaps already—am I to think he can't have enchanted this *very* (Jock said) pretty courier of his? He has been in Paris a fortnight. Do these American girls resist as long as that? *Has* this one resisted?—a man like him? Am I to ask Jock?

As if what matter!

Or bother my *head* whether this is the, the recurring scenario I know it of course must be! For how straightforward, how classical even, I thought, looking at him—you could have met me and voilà, simply decided that I enchant you more than she. Even much more —I am a dagger glittering to its mark. But what are weapons? A heart like yours who can think herself the last and deadliest to wound! . . .

—Ah mais tu es *à moi!* (I said to him in my mind), and here in this gay room, this place of flowers and light, place now of my lovely freedom again too, you are mine to tease, mon américain de re- change—for truly perhaps you *are* so desperate that you are being honest, libertine or not. And if you are, think: *really* can you never have guessed what happened to me that morning? when I turned round in Chad's car and saw you for what alas you are, the sun in your blue eyes, the wind fluttering your tie....

—Of course shall I ever be sure.

For how could the sort of man *you* are, mon Sather, have been so bold, or had the effrontery or the mere cynicism to think I would sit and listen, unless you . . . *more* than hoped you knew I would want to?

I shall never be sure. But then, hoh, shall I ever have to let *you* be sure either!

So now? à la fin? à la longue?

A la fin you are mine whenever I want to take the Dionysiac risk of you and your beguiling Paris office-to-be; and I said, "But mon Dieu, Mr. Sather, how can you expect me to advise you? . . ." and let my eyes smile.

A NOTE ABOUT THE AUTHOR

W. M. Spackman was born in Coatesville, Pennsylvania. He is a graduate of the Friends School in Wilmington, Delaware, and of Princeton University, and he was also a Rhodes scholar at Balliol College, Oxford. He is the author of three previous novels, *Heyday* (1953), *An Armful of Warm Girl* (1978), and *A Presence with Secrets* (1980), as well as a collection of critical essays, *On the Decay of Humanism* (1967).

A NOTE ON THE TYPE

This book was set on the Linotype in Granjon, a type named after Robert Granjon. George W. Jones based his designs for this type upon that used by Claude Garamond (c. 1480–1561) in his beautiful French books. Granjon more closely resembles Garamond's own type than do the various modern types that bear his name. Robert Granjon began his career as type cutter in 1523 and was one of the first to practice the trade of type founder apart from that of printer.

Composed by the Maryland Linotype Composition Co., Baltimore, Maryland
Printed and bound by R. R. Donnelley & Sons Co., Harrisonburg, Virgina

Typography by Joe Marc Freedman